BIGFOOT'S CURSE

A CREATURE FEATURE BY MICHAEL COLE

BIGFOOT'S CURSE

www.severedpress.com

ISBN: 978-1-923165-92-2

CHAPTER 1

It only took about twenty minutes to get to the gates. For Spencer, it felt like a hundred years. That piece of rock—in his opinion, it was made of rock—in his kidney felt as if it had a mind of its own. And in that evil mind was an evil intent, and that was to cause him great pain and misery.

Ned pointed to a fork in the road. "Just up this way. Follow the little trail and we'll find the place."

"The place'." Spencer stuck his tongue out. "Who the hell would want to build an expensive science building all the way out here?"

"Why don't you ask when we come through the gates?" Ned said.

Spencer groaned in indifference and discomfort, steering the vehicle through the narrow pathway.

"You know, if they had so much money to spend on lab stuff, they could at least have done some work on the trail here, instead of requiring us to get a new paint job for our truck every time we ship to them."

Ned tightened his lips and nodded. "Yeah, can't argue that." He watched the glow of the headlights reach through the grid of the fence. "Ah-ha! We're here."

Spencer pulled up closer, then eased on the brake.

"Um… does it usually look like this?"

Ned sat quietly, first looking at the broken section of fence to their right. 'Broken' didn't do it justice; 'torn apart' was a little more accurate. A whole twelve-foot section had been torn off and ripped to pieces, which lay scattered about in the grass.

"No. It does not."

Spencer blew the horn and stuck his head out the window. "Hello? Is anyone there?" His voice traveled far into the distance.

Nobody answered.

"Now many people are usually here?" he asked Ned.

"Thirteen staff, overall. There's the head doctor, some lab assistants, some people to help maintain the machines. There's always someone in the little guard shack when they're expecting a shipment."

Spencer looked at the little cube-shaped building on the other side of the gate. "Nobody there now." He squinted. "Can't really see past it."

"Take us through that opening," Ned said, pointing at the breach in the fence. Spencer gave thought to arguing against that. Whatever was going on here, he wanted no part of it. But Ned outranked him, and with the pain from the kidney stone, he had no stamina for arguing.

"Alright."

He backed the propane truck up a few feet, then steered it through the gap.

PLUSH!

The truck bumped.

"Oh, shit."

Ned lowered his head and groaned. "I said drive through the opening. Not blow a tire by running over a piece of bent metal."

"Motherfucker, I couldn't see it. Something tells me *you* wouldn't have seen it either. Not that I care, because I'm in pain!"

He limped the vehicle through the perimeter and steered it back onto the little roadway, where he placed it in park.

Both men immediately forgot about the flattened tire after seeing the wreckage that used to be a very high-tech facility.

"I don't suppose it usually looks like this, either?" Spencer said.

Ned's jaw dropped. "No."

He stepped outside and gave a look at the place. The main building, located up ahead on the left, was leaning to the south, its foundation heavily compromised by what looked like an intense blow from a charging rhino. There was a gaping hole in its west end, with debris scattered over the roadway.

In the middle of that mess was the flattened body of a man in a lab coat.

"Oh, my God."

"Let's get out of here," Spencer said.

"We have to see if anybody's still alive," Ned argued.

Spencer was gritting his teeth and bumping his fist repeatedly against the hood of their truck. "Nobody's alive, I can tell you that right now!"

Ned dismissed his words as the kidney stone talking, and went forward. "Hello? Hel—"

He looked to the dome-shaped structure to the right, measuring maybe forty feet from east to west, and only ten feet in height. Part of its roof was peeled open, as though something had burst out of it.

That description may have been more than a simile, based on the wet trail in the concrete and bent grass, leading to a burrowed tunnel *under* that portion of the gate. Whatever had broken out of that dome had escaped the premises and entered into the small cove, which fed into Lake Shire.

"Holy shit!"

Ned jumped, not expecting Spencer to be right there. He ignored the tendency to curse at his driving partner to further examine the ruins of the company facility.

He did not know much about the Rain Corporation, aside that they designed products, like every other company. He didn't even question why they had a research lab all the way out here, or why hardly anyone knew about it. The place itself was not even clearly marked. The signs just read Private Property. Only a handful of contractors, such as themselves, were even aware Rain owned this spot of land. It was out of the way for the most part, easily missed by anyone who hiked around here.

"Something was in there," Spencer said.

"Yeah." Ned spoke barely above a whisper.

"What was it? You think it did all of this?" Spencer gestured at the wreckage around them.

Ned shook his head. "No. Whatever was in there, it went straight for the lake." He looked at the damage to the lab building and other structures. There were a few trailers used for crew quarters, a recreation building, and a radio shack. "Something *else* did all this."

Spencer panned his eyes across the place, freezing after pointing them at something lying between.

"Something like that?"

Ned saw it too. He stiffened, afraid that any movement would awaken the thing, presuming it was asleep. It was as large as a Buick and white as snow, aside from a long pinkish thing that stretched from its end well into the grass.

Taking one step at a time, the two drivers approached, stopping after realizing what it was.

"Jes—" Spencer spasmed, the stress and kidney stone working hand-in-hand. "That's a rat."

"Two rats." Ned ignited a flashlight and aimed it at another white animal of equal size lying on the other side of the road. Because of the trees, they had missed it when they first came in, even though it stuck out like a sore thumb. This one, they could see its face. Its eyes were black as marbles, its mouth sporting large teeth. Its claws were bent at the knuckles, its body rigid.

From the corner of its mouth dripped a now coagulated river of blood.

"It's dead," Ned said. He was half-relieved, but still stricken with tension. Seeing a rat as big as a car, even a dead one, would haunt his nightmares for years.

"What were these people working on?" Spencer said in a gasping voice. He looked again at the main building. "Good GOD! What *were* they working on?!"

Ned looked for himself. With the help of a flashlight, he was able to see what had Spencer worked up.

He thought giant rats were bad enough. But this? This took it to a whole new level.

A giant spiderweb, stretching between a tree and the end of one of the trailers, waved in the breeze. Scattered about were five funnel-shaped objects, approximately six feet from top to bottom. Each one had two tiny blue reflections when the light hit them.

Eyes.

Human eyes.

That realization, and the sight of multilegged organisms moving in the corner of the nest, made Ned lower the flashlight and backpedal to the truck.

"Good God! Let's get the hell out of here!"

Spencer's pain elevated once more. "See what happens when you don't listen to me? I wanted to turn around and get out of here."

"Yeah, yeah, shut up." Ned went to get a closer look at the gate.

"What are you doing?" Spencer said.

"Just wanted to make sure there's nothing else we'd run over. We only have three good tires. I—"

Both men looked at the gap in the fence. In the faint reach of the light was a humanoid form standing in it, shoulders hunched, its chest rising and falling.

Its basic shape was the only thing it had in similarity to the human species. Everything else was pure animal. Not even animal… *monster.*

Two orange eyes reflected the light. Its body appeared to be a dark brown, its height falling just short of the fifteen-foot fence.

Ned backed away. "That isn't there. I'm just seeing things."

The thing moved into the glow of his torch. Its face, ape-like, diseased, and rotted on the left side, bared razor-sharp teeth.

It strutted onto the property, its beathing intensifying with sharp exhales.

Ned dropped the light and made a run to the truck. “No-no-no-no-no!”

It quickened its pace and intercepted him with a mighty grab. Ned was lifted off the ground and held high over its head.

“Agh! Put me do—ARGGGGHHH!”

One of those hands closed over his head, muffling him. The other grabbed him by his legs. Together, they bent him down.

Crack—SPLAT!

His abdomen burst, his spine breaking like a dry twig, shooting blood and guts like water from a balloon.

Spencer’s head began to spin. What he was looking at was beyond reality. He had seen it on television, in books, and on the internet.

At best, it was fun speculation. For the most part, it was the subject of entertainment and fictional stories.

But it was real, and the horror fiction depicting it on television proved far more accurate than any of the documentaries and journals could ever dream to be.

Bigfoot existed, and he was violent.

It dropped Ned’s two halves and came at him.

Spencer turned to run. The pain in his side flared to levels he didn’t think were possible.

He fell to his knees, his kidney feeling as though it would burst out of him.

The ground rumbled.

"Please, don't! Leave me alone!"

There was no reasoning with the beast. It viewed humans as both food and a threat. Having been contained in this human-made facility, with vile processed foods to serve as nourishment, it leaned heavily on the 'threat' viewpoint.

It lifted Spencer off the ground with one hand. With the other, it chose to get creative.

Spencer gagged, the thumb and index finger driving their sharp nails into his side. He spat blood, then grunted as those pinched digits ripped outward, carrying much of his insides with them.

Looking him dead in the eye, it put those innards in its mouth. It chewed, savoring the raw taste.

Crunch!

Bigfoot winced, then spat them out. Near its foot was Spencer's chewed up kidney, with a pebble-shaped object rolling out of it.

He had gotten his wish: that kidney stone was removed.

It didn't help the pain any. What did help was having his head smashed against a tree.

Being dead had a unique way of alleviating pain and misery.

CHAPTER 2

The sun was shining bright, warming the town of Southgate and the residents within. It was an eighty-five-degree day, and it was only eleven in the morning. In three hours, it would go up to ninety-five.

Every winter, Bradford could hardly think of anything else except for his winter trips. Then it came time to leave for them, and he would find himself wondering why he was so eager. As much as he didn't want to admit it, he was very much an average twenty-first century guy. He depended heavily on his air conditioning during the months of June, July, and August. Otherwise, any sort of relaxation, especially sleep, was impossible.

It was a thought that always made him question if he could stand being in a tent these days. Even worse, it had been a few years since they last went out to the Wiregrass Forest. Every trip since 2019 had been in a hotel, which was kept nice and cool at night, enabling him to sleep under the weight of three blankets. At this point in life, he was reliant on such conditioning.

One time, the a/c unit broke down, and for two weeks, he and his wife had to suffer without it. Even with four fans in his bedroom, he could not get comfortable. It was as though the house had become a microwave.

In his early years of marriage to his wife Heather, he had joked a few times about how he ought to sleep naked. Of course, there was sexual context to that joke. In actuality, he had gotten so hot during that period of time that he sweated through most of his pajamas. Being so uncomfortable, he actually resorted to sleeping in his birthday suit, much to Heather's amusement.

Unfortunately, unlike those old jokes, it didn't lead to anything fun. They were both in their early forties now. Their kids were the ages of eight, nine, and twelve. The youngest was a surprise, conceived during the last remnants of a time when things were constantly hot and heavy between Bradford and Heather Wynn.

They still loved each other and had no plans for separation. Even if they did, neither of them would initiate such a move while the kids were still young. They were just used to each other.

Maybe too much so.

As Bradford packed the truck, he got a glimpse of the old Dodge Durango parked near the garage. It was old and in heavy need of repairs. Heather had made a few remarks about scrapping it. On a technical note, she was correct. It was no good, and the repairs needed would cost more than the car was worth.

But Bradford couldn't bring himself to do it. There were too many memories in that car; memories he and Heather used to reminisce about. One of the best ones was while they were engaged. They were in their twenties at the time, both living with their parents with very little privacy. So, they snuck away with his Durango to 'get some takeout'.

They did, in fact go to a restaurant… to park behind it, where they flattened the back seats, and had a good time in the trunk.

The few times he brought it up, Heather would give a mild grin. Bradford wasn't sure if she had grown too mature for those antics, or just didn't care anymore.

He feared it was because she didn't want to think of when he was younger and hotter. Bradford was still healthy, but like with all people, time was doing its thing. His hair was starting to thin, his abs were gone, and there was a little more arthritis in his joints. Nothing that prevented him from being active, but age was taking its natural toll. That, and his lack of going to the gym.

Looking at his faint reflection in the truck window, he thought of the guy he was when they dated and got married. Tan, lean, good muscle tone, and thick hair. It was definitely not the guy he was looking at there. Seeing himself in the actual mirror was worse, and he would not dare look at photos of himself.

Bradford, practicing armchair psychology, wondered if he was going through the dreaded midlife crisis. He didn't have any desires to go off and do foolish things to prove he was still young at heart. He just hated the natural decline that came with the passing of years. Deep down, he knew focusing on it was wasted energy, but the subconscious was a powerful force.

Did Heather see the same ugly thing he saw? Was she no longer attracted to him, hence the sharp decrease in physical affection? He would have argued that this trip would have been an opportunity for them to get wild with each other once again, except she had invited another married couple to camp out with them.

Separate tents, of course, but it still intruded on the potential for steamy moments.

"Okay, guys, be good for your Aunt Annette's house, alright? Okay, love you all. Bye!" Heather closed the door behind her and started walking to the truck. "Okay, Brad. Kids are happy. They're getting pizza tonight. Extra cheese."

Bradford smiled and tapped his belly. "I tend to be guilty of such things myself from time to time."

"Uh-huh." She went around to the passenger side and got in the cab, leaving Bradford feeling awkward near his door.

He pulled himself inside and started it up. "Shawn and Betty still coming?"

"Yes," she said in a long, drawn-out voice. "I think that's the third time you've asked. You not like them or something?"

"They're okay," he said. "Shawn and I get along just fine. You and Betty seem happy drinking wine together and talking about the firm."

"Ah, yes," she said with a chuckle. "The place that should not be named."

Bradford pretended to laugh at that remark. Deep down, his self-consciousness was kicking his ass. Bradford, the former karate practitioner who could run a five-forty-five mile and bench three-hundred pounds, and had ambitions of becoming a doctor was an out-of-shape parcel delivery driver. Heather, an aspiring lawyer, settled for being a legal secretary at a local firm. They were almost literally Doug and Carrie from *The King of Queens*. A few extra pounds, he would match his on-screen counterpart, just not as funny.

That was another thing: he was fast with the jokes and one-liners. Maybe it was a testosterone thing. Since he quit exercising and fell into the routine of adulting, he gradually lost his 'edge' when it came to that stuff.

"You okay?" Heather asked.

Bradford snapped out of his self-loathing trance. "Oh! Yeah, sorry, got lost in thought."

"Okay. You know, you can talk to me if anything's bothering you, right?"

"Of course," he replied. She nodded, seemingly satisfied with his response. Bradford maintained the facade of contentment as he backed out of the driveway and began the drive to Wiregrass Forest.

It was vacation time!

For most people, it was an occasion to be jovial. Bradford, on the other hand, was already missing the comfort of his own bed.

CHAPTER 3

The time was 10:45 a.m. when Trenton Loar pulled up to the gate. There were two men in suits standing guard, resembling secret service personnel protecting an elected official. As usual, the one with the big mustache approached the window of Trenton's car.

"Identification, please."

Trenton handed it over. The guy had seen him a hundred times by now, and knew he was scheduled to appear, and yet he always followed procedure to the letter. In a sense, Trenton couldn't blame the guy, as he had done jobs where every 't' needed crossed and every 'i' dotted.

While Mustache Guard took his sweet time, Trenton looked past the gate at the big mansion. It was a place he had gone through many times, even the boiler rooms and underground tunnels. He had been part of the crime lord Ennio Vogler's security team for many years now, having consulted in fortifying the mansion, as well as executing several off-site operations. In the world of narcotics, there was little room for ethics. He had single-handedly taken out competitors, shaken up supply lines, and even managed to get some DEA agents off Ennio's back in a way that did not raise questions. Trenton knew how to sneak into a house and an apartment, and the internet was a useful tool. His favorite method was to hang someone in front of a laptop with illicit material on the screen. Leaving no trace, fingerprints or otherwise, he left investigators with little else to go on.

Other jobs were messier, generally the ones that involved the bringing down of shipments from competing operations. Trenton always believed in striking first. In this business, if one didn't make the first move, they were making themselves vulnerable to the enemy.

It was a philosophy Trenton lived by to this day. That, and studying everyone you believed to be a threat… including your friends.

That philosophy brought him here today… all under the guise of business, of course.

Mustache Guard handed him his ID back. "Pull over to the third lot."

"Mmhmm."

It was as if the guy was an AI bot, repeating the same actions and phrases day in and day out.

The gate opened, and Trenton went to his usual spot. It was in front of the main entrance to the mansion. Two guards in business casual outfits stood in the blistering sun, their sunglasses a poor prop in their efforts to look intimidating.

He stepped out of his car and moved to the door, opening his jacket to assure he was not carrying. As indicated by their attire, these guys were a little more casual, nodding their approval at him and letting him through the doors. In actuality, they should've patted him down. In a way, it made Trenton respect Mustache Guard's adherence to procedure, for these guys did not follow the philosophy of always being prepared.

As he approached the doors, Trenton glanced to his right. A hundred feet or so in that direction was a fourth lot, with two inconspicuous vehicles owned by Ennio's staff. In spite of the extravagant home and lifestyle, Ennio was savvy enough to know many aspects of the business needed to *not* be eye-catching. They were smuggling cocaine and crystal meth. Many eyes were constantly on Ennio—he was used to that aspect by now. The lawyers were always good at finding alibis and loopholes to keep him beyond the reach of the law. But running a business like this had a lot of moving parts, and any of them could potentially be traced back to the mansion.

Those cars were new, not in year, but in ownership by the staff members; exactly as Trenton suggested.

He entered the mansion and found the stairway at the end of the main hall. He went up to the second floor and went east, passing a large balcony overlooking a wide living room area. It was a setup so similar to a certain movie from the 80s, Trenton suspected it was directly inspired from it. Down there were five men, all armed with automatic pistols.

Suitable, considering...

By the doors was a guard.

"Trenton Loar?"

"That's me."

The guard opened the door.

Behind it was a huge office, complete with lush furniture that cost more than most average people made in a year. The desk was U-shaped and covered in a tight layer of crocodile leather.

Seated behind it, smoking a fat cigar, was Ennio Vogler. He was bald, wore an open white shirt exposing his potbelly and hairy chest, and had his feet crossed on the edge of his desk. With nothing else going on in the room, Trenton knew it was all for show. Otherwise, the guy was literally just sitting in here looking like a villain in a children's cartoon all by himself all morning.

Then again, knowing Ennio, there was a possibility that was true.

"Mr. Loar. Well done on the Whitehead job. Funds have been wired to your account."

Trenton maintained his usual boring demeanor. It was too hard to fake a smile with Ennio today. No matter how rich and powerful he was, the grudge which led him here was too much.

"It's what I do," he replied.

"Pull up a chair," Ennio said. "Want a cigar?"

"Chair, no thank you. Cigar? Absolutely."

Ennio pointed his thumb to the right side of the room, directing Trenton to help himself. He went to a large wooden cabinet located beside a giant steel lockbox.

He pulled out a Honduran cigar, bit its end off, and lit its tip with a match.

"Whiskey?" Ennio offered.

"Just one, thank you." Trenton moved to the chair. Ennio filled a five-ounce glass and pushed it over to him. Trenton downed the golden fluid and returned to puffing on the stogie.

"I'm glad you're here," Ennio said. "I've got another job for you. You might be happy to know it'll be easier than the Whitehead assignment. Though, a trigger will have to be pulled. But you already know that, I'm sure." He handed over a tan folder. "That's not to say there won't be risk, and it's definitely not to say it's not an incredibly important task. Hence, I'm offering you double the usual rate. Now, for the details…"

"Ah, yes, the details," Trenton said.

Ennio chuckled nervously, not used to this sort of tone from his trusted assassin. "I know you value intel…"

"I do. Especially my own."

Ennio's smile dropped. He pulled the cigar from his mouth.

"Excuse me?"

Trenton pulled out his own picture. On it was a scrawny man in a brown shirt and sunglasses.

Ennio pretended to be surprised. "Who's this?"

"What? You don't remember your mole in the DEA? The one you were planning on giving me up to?"

A vein inflated in Ennio's forehead.

"You think me a fool? Handing you over to the DEA would only give them leverage to dig into my business. You think I want that?"

"No, but that nephew of yours has a big mouth," Trenton said. He watched Ennio's tan complexion turn a pale shade. "He did some singing last time he got arrested, specifically about the hit in New Orleans. You know, the one on the agent who was investigating him. They don't have my real name, but they believe they can connect it to you if they dig deeper. Your mole told you, and you guys had to come up with a clever plan to get the agency off your back. Best way to do that? Set me up for a trap."

Ennio was not sure if he was frightened or impressed. He knew of Trenton's philosophy of keeping tabs on everyone, but now that his expertise had been utilized on him and his allies, he realized how dedicated the assassin was to his methods.

Very quickly, his feelings swayed to frightened, remembering what the precise and dedicated Trenton Loar did to people he considered a threat. If he thought the president of the United States wanted his head, Trenton would tear through the entire White House and every bunker on the planet until he got him.

Ennio was starting to sweat. Behind those wide eyes was a mind wishing the crime lord was in his own bunker.

There was no negotiating beyond this point.

Ennio went for the gun under his desk.

Trenton lifted his leg and drew from his concealed ankle holster the guards at the front door were too lazy to check for. Two shots pierced Ennio's chest.

The crime lord jolted in his chair, mouth wide open, arms out, eyes looking down at the blood pooling onto his belly. They went back to the smoking muzzle and the blank stare behind it.

Trenton didn't waste time with one-liners. It'd be the same one most times. *"This is why you strike first."*

He fired a third shot. Ennio's head whipped back, the brow inflated to make room for the expansion of his skull after the bullet punched through.

The doors opened behind Trenton. He turned around and fired two shots into the guard, dropping him. Beyond the balcony, he could hear other guards shouting to one another about shots being fired.

Trenton wasn't worried about their advantage in numbers. Many of them hadn't fired a shot in their entire career. Trenton did it all the time, almost entirely at living targets.

All he needed to even the score were better tools. Fortunately, he had used his many talents to learn the code to Ennio's lockbox well in advance. He opened the doors and took in the pleasant sight of several military-grade assault rifles.

It was in this moment Trenton cracked a smile. Somehow, he knew Ennio would have an M16 assault rifle with an underbarrel grenade launcher. Maybe this mansion was partially designed with a specific purpose, and with the fantasy of a particular standoff taking place. Ennio was the type to consider the fact that said standoff didn't end well for the special character.

Trenton had a different outcome in mind. Unlike Al Pacino's *Scarface*, he would make it out of this mansion.

Several footsteps approached the doors.

Trenton turned to his right and pointed a freshly loaded M16. A burst of ammunition cut through two of the guards attempting to storm the office. The others frantically shut the doors, hoping to box him in.

Now, the tough-as-nails assassin was chuckling. He was often calm in shootouts. Generally, his best performance was when he shut all emotion out. But this time, he allowed himself to experience the joy and humor. How could he not? They had literally set him up for an imitation of the big line.

Even better, many of them were grouped right outside the door.

"This is too good," he said. Loading the grenade launcher, he crouched slightly and pointed it at the door. *"Say hello to my little friend!"*

BOOM!

Six men screamed as they were tossed from the flash of fire and wood fragments. Three of them were on the carpet, numb from the concussion, attempting to crawl away. The other three were in pieces, joining their employer in hell.

Trenton hugged the wall and approached the doorway. More guards were gathering in the lobby and were making their way up various staircases to get to the balcony.

He leaned out the door, gun-first, and unleashed a spray to the side. One guard, who had been silently approaching, caught three rounds in the chest. Others who were farther back, retreated to the stairs, accidentally bunching up. A single grenade took all five of them out in bloody fashion.

Trenton swung his rifle to the other direction, spraying bullets into a group of frightened guards coming at him. A few shots streaked his way, all going wide. Blood splattered, the hot lead ravaging their flesh like chainsaws.

Next, he made sure to fire a few shots at the guards down in the lobby. One took a round in the right side of his chest, putting him into a wild spin as he sprayed his own gun, accidentally taking out two of his comrades.

Trenton fired a third grenade. The blast was dark, lifting granite, pieces of furniture, and one of the men off the floor.

He retreated into the office, knowing they would hold back for another minute before making another rush at him. It was the perfect opportunity to exercise the next part of his plan.

First, he placed a plastic explosive on Ennio's lap. Knowing his personnel, they would swarm their leader like knights to a king, even after seeing the gaping hole in his forehead.

Next, he pulled out his coiled black rope from his side pocket. He went to the outside balcony, taking a quick look to see how many men were down there. As he anticipated, there were a small handful. Most of them were flooding the building, believing he would try to escape through the elevators and hallways.

"Good morning!" he called down to the trio.

They looked up and shared the same look of surprise after seeing the grenade launcher pointed at them.

BOOM!

It was a hell of a treat. Trenton was enjoying himself for once. Part of it was because this particular gunfight was personal. Ennio had intended to kill him, after all. Every shootout he had been in prior had been business related.

He fast-roped down to the concrete. After touching down, his attention went to the balcony he had dropped from. Multiple armed personnel were assembling, having drawn up the courage to infiltrate the room.

"He's down here!" one shouted, pointing at him.

Trenton pulled his detonator, extended its antenna, and pressed the button.

This *BOOM* made the grenade explosions look like fire crackers. A ball of fire extended from the back of the mansion, throwing the smoldering bodies of Ennio's henchmen across the lawn.

Deep within the structure, many other shouts of panic echoed. Ceilings had collapsed throughout, causing all sorts of chaos.

He went around the building. Near the corner was one guard standing watch.

Trenton took him down with an elbow to the face and the slamming of the rifle butt on his throat, dispatching him silently.

Afterwards, he continued navigating his path through the property. Eventually, he arrived in the front lot.

"There!" one of the guards shouted. It was the one who failed to frisk him.

Trenton drew first, putting a round through his neck. The partner moved to the side, throwing off his own aim as he returned fire. Trenton, keeping calm, put several rounds through his abdomen, nearly sawing him in half.

Reloading his mag, he ran to the cars he saw in Lot Four, gunning down two more guards on his way.

Arriving at the passenger side of the black one, he opened the door and rolled down the window.

In the driver's seat was Matt Bing, Ennio's personal driver.

"Damn! You actually made it out!"

"Shut up and drive," Trenton said, extending the rifle out the window.

Matt shifted the lever to drive and pulled up his two-way radio. "Jerry? Carl? You guys set?"

"Ready when you are. Charges have been set, exactly as Loar instructed."

"Perfect. Our new boss says you're up."

"Here we go."

Another explosion tore the gate apart, clearing the way for their escape.

Matt floored the accelerator, speeding them through the newly created gap. With the wind in his hair, Trenton watched the window, catching a glimpse of Mustache Guard's charred face as he lay dead several yards away from where he had been standing. Interestingly, that big ol' mustache somehow managed to remain untouched.

"Okay! We're out!" the fifth member of their group, Billy Howard, announced from the blue car behind them. *"We need to head north. We'll dump the vehicles in the river, collect our new transport, and head to the woods. If we act fast, they'll lose our trail."*

Trenton watched the smoke rising from the mansion in the rearview mirror. Hopefully his navigator was as good as his reputation suggested. Trenton may have deleted one opponent, but in doing so, he created many more. His funds had been withdrawn and he had a plan in place to fake his death. All he needed to do was stay out of sight. Considering himself a less than social individual, that wasn't asking for much.

For now, all he could do was follow the plan and hope everything was literally as simple as a walk in the woods.

In their case, it was the thick woods of Wiregrass Forest.

CHAPTER 4

It was as beautiful as Bradford and Heather remembered. Wiregrass Forest was a large natural park that was largely left untouched by modern man. A few trails had been paved some time in the 1970s, but overall, the only people who came through here were hikers, fishermen, and campers. Aside from one small spot on the north end of the lake that was purchased by a private company, it was all considered private land.

For most of the drive, Heather was back and forth between a paperback and her smartphone. When they entered the woods, she was forced to rely on the paperback for her entertainment, as any internet signal was quickly lost.

"Don't think we're alone out here," Bradford said.

Heather, not looking up from her book, chuckled. "I wouldn't think so. Plenty of people tend to camp out here. It's a big place."

Bradford rolled his eyes. "Alright, yes. I was referring to these motorcycles here."

She looked over at a group of Harley Davidsons chained to a bunch of trees. There were ten of them, the one on the end mounted with a small sign.

Touch our bikes and see what happens. There was a picture of a baseball bat and chain, with a red scribble underneath them.

"That supposed to be blood?" she said.

Bradford snorted. "I think it is." He exaggerated a look of intense fear. "Ooo! I'm so frightened. I might get beat up by a bunch of people with crayons!"

"Hey, don't joke," Heather said. "Guys like those come straight out of a stereotypical 80's shoot 'em up. They might mean trouble."

"You want us to head home?" Bradford asked.

"No, that's not what I'm saying," she replied. "I'm just saying, don't underestimate those kinds of people." She tapped his belly in a way that was meant to be loving, but for him, only felt derogatory. "You haven't been in a fight in, what, twelve years? If you can even call them fights, being light-contact sparring sessions with referees."

Bradford wrinkled his nose, those playful words providing ample ammunition for the self-consciousness that plagued his mind.

"For your information, we went full contact in the dojo. Our sensei was old-school."

"I know." Heather laughed again. "That's why you had to get two crowns." She put a finger to his jaw, where he had absorbed the full velocity of a spinning heel kick.

"Well… you should've seen the other guy," he quipped.

Heather went back to her book. "I'm sure you had him on the ropes, honey."

Bradford continued driving. He knew she didn't mean anything by it, but those damn intrusive thoughts were going to work on him.

Yeah, I think it is a midlife crisis.

It was thirty minutes later when they came to a bend in the thin trail which led to their usual campground. From afar, they could see Shawn and Betty's orange Dodge Journey parked near the tree with the bent trunk. Somehow, the giant plant had a malfunction in its growth at some point, causing it to lean heavily to the east.

It was a moment Bradford and Heather expected to get washed with nostalgia at the place where they had gone on their first trip as a couple, got engaged, tried out all sorts of different hiking equipment, amongst many other great memories.

Instead, they both were taken aback at the sight of three motorcycles propped a few feet away from the Dodge Journey.

In the small clearing was Shawn and Betty Menger, dressed in typical summer clothes, going toe-to-toe with a man in a black leather vest, a big earing dangling from his left lobe, a cheap pair of sunglasses, and a tiny grey goatee on his chin.

Two other bikers accompanied the guy. From what Bradford and Heather could see, they did not have any weapons in hand. But that didn't mean things were not about to get ugly. And basic body language indicated the temperature was getting hot, and not just from the afternoon sunshine.

"Oh, great!" Heather said. "What a great start to this trip."

"Either these guys are out for trouble, or Shawn decided to be daring with one of their bikes," Bradford replied.

"I don't think these are the same guys from the group we saw back there," Heather said. "We probably would've seen them pass us."

"You might be right, but it's safe to assume they're part of the same outfit." Bradford parked their vehicle, keeping the engine running as he stepped out.

Shawn, a man in his early thirties with a physique earned from regular visits to the gym, scowled at the leader of the biker trio.

"Oh, you want some?"

"You asked for it," the biker guy said.

"Yeah?" Betty said. "You guys think you own the place?"

She had red highlights in her hair and wore a loose tank top. As much as Bradford tried not to look, it was difficult, even now, to not notice the lack of a bra underneath.

Some friends Heather invited.

Betty was just as feisty as her husband, and more than happy to see him clash with the biker guy.

"Whoa! Whoa! Whoa!" Bradford approached with his hands raised. "Let's not get too carried away, shall we? I'm sure this is all a big misunderstanding…"

"Who asked you, Cheesecake?" the biker guy spat.

Bradford stopped, the tremors of anxiety rocking his body fast and hard. All of a sudden, he totally agreed with Heather's earlier implication about him not doing well in a fight.

When in doubt, resort to humor.

"Well, I should lay off the butter." He laughed, hoping it would catch on with the rest of the crowd.

It didn't.

The biker's eyes went back to Shawn. "This is our spot."

"You have no ownership of this place," Betty shouted.

"Our bikes were here!" one of the other bikers said.

"They were over *there*." Shawn pointed to a spot several yards to the north.

"Yeah," the leader said. "This is all our territory."

Shawn turned away, laughing at the absurdity of the comment. The guy was seriously talking about these woods as though it was some urban area with all kinds of illicit business.

"Redneck bikers. I gotta love it," he remarked.

The leader was not loving it. He moved forward and shoved Shawn backwards.

"Hey! Hey! Hey!" Bradford exclaimed. He promptly stopped as the other two rednecks strutted in his direction.

The leader shoved Shawn a second time, pushing him up against Betty.

Shawn retaliated with a right hook that caught the guy on the chin. He stumbled backward, caught off guard by the blow.

"Let's go!" Shawn said.

The leader reached into his back pocket and revealed a switchblade. "Alright, bitch."

Shawn grimaced at the weapon, not sure why he was surprised that the scumbag was not up for a fair fight.

Betty, seemingly having retreated to their vehicle, reemerged with something to even the score. Chambering a round of her forty-caliber Smith & Wesson, she quickly gave the bikers reason to back away from her man.

"I've been dying to use this," she said. "Usually, I fantasize about my dumbass boss and some of my coworkers being in front of this thing. But you guys are more than satisfactory for my violent temper."

The biker leader, still holding his switchblade, slowly backed away.

"Listen, bitch," he said to her. "You're picking a fight you can't win."

"That's right," one of his guys parroted.

"I don't think you even know how to use that thing," the third remarked.

BANG!

All three of them jumped at the burst of sound and the small explosion of dirt near the leader's feet.

He pointed a finger at her. "Just you wait." He forced a sinister laugh, then retreated to his bike.

All three of them roared their engines and hooked around, traveling far into the woods.

Betty lowered the gun and whistled. "That certainly gets the heart going, doesn't it."

Shawn walked over to her and planted a big wet kiss on her mouth. "We sent them packing, didn't we?"

She grabbed him hard and resumed the make out session.

Bradford, meanwhile, was catching his breath. Heather wasn't doing much better. They had come out here to get away from all the bullshit they saw in so-called civilization, not get dragged into some feud.

She stepped out of the vehicle. "Everyone alright?"

Betty and Shawn were definitely alright. By the looks of it, the whole encounter got them all buttered up for some hot action.

Bradford looked to his wife. "You know, it's not too late to turn around and head to the casino." He winked. "You love the mattresses they have in the hotel."

"Yeah, and you love the hot-tub," she retorted, much to the amusement of their fellow couple.

After a few more moments of hot and heavy passion, Shawn separated from Betty and walked over to the Wynns.

"Bradford! Haven't seen you in a while!"

"Hey Shawn." They shook hands. "I see you got your workout in today."

Shawn laughed. "Those guys' bark is worse than their bite. They like to push people around, but once they get a little taste of their own medicine, they scatter like roaches."

"This helps a tad," Betty quipped, sporting her pistol.

Bradford nodded. He had considered packing his own home-defense firearm, but ultimately chose not to. Back in the day, he loved going to the range and to his parent's backyard, where he would shoot watermelons. But it had been a long while since he had pulled a trigger.

"It certainly does," he replied. "I see you've got your tent set up already. You guys think we should stay here, or should we pick another spot?"

"Nah!" Shawn brushed his shoulder. "We sent them packing. Like I said, they're cowards. They're not gonna risk getting a third eyeball."

Bradford tilted his head north. "Yeah, but they're part of a larger group we saw…"

"All a bunch of sissies," Shawn interrupted. "They think because they wear leather and drive bikes that they're a bunch of tough guys. Worst part is, most people fall for it. They're used to pushing people around, but like I said, when someone pushes back, they scatter."

"Yeah, but they only scattered when they saw the gun," Bradford said. "Up until then, they seemed pretty willing to escalate things with a knife."

"He wasn't gonna use it," Betty said.

"And what if the others have guns?" Bradford continued.

"Holy smokes!" Shawn burst out laughing. "We scared them off right in front of you, man." He looked at Heather. "Get your puppy some treats and a belly rub! That might settle him down."

Heather forced a smile. "Yeah, I think it'll be fine." She chuckled nervously. "I was gonna crack open a Pepsi, but right now, I don't think my heart could benefit from caffeine."

"Yeah." Having lost the argument, Bradford moved to their truck. "I guess I'll start setting up the tent."

"Don't worry, guys, I'm sure that's the worst of it," Shawn said in a proud and sure voice.

"God-willing," Bradford said, lifting some gear from the truck. "I'd hate for things to get *too* exciting on this trip."

CHAPTER 5

The switchblade twirled through the air until its tip embedded into the trunk of a tree. Still furious at the recent encounter, Redge Canty strutted to the tree and yanked his knife free. Envisioning that tough-guy and his hot but bitchy wife on the business end of that blade was only mildly therapeutic.

"Those shiteaters," he growled. He looked at his two pals, Joe and Hunter, nodding in agreement. "You see how that hotshot pulled a gun on me? Thinking she's hot shit or something." He growled like a wild animal and rubbed his hands together. "I've never hit a woman in my life…"

"Well…" Joe cleared his throat. "There was Marcy."

Redge thought about it. "Okay, sure. One simple backhand to the face. No big deal. Other than her…"

"And Kate," Hunter added.

Redge stopped. "Right. Kate. Other than those two… I've never—"

"And Merrin," Joe said.

"Will you guys quit!" he shouted. "My point is, that piece of tail is well on her way to being added to my list."

"Yeah! That's right!" Joe mindlessly declared.

"We'll show her," Hunter added. He sniffed, in need of an extra whiff of the special treat stuffed in his pocket. "How should we do it? Wanna go back tonight?" He cracked a smile. "Want me to film it? You know? *It?*"

Redge knew what the junkie had on his mind. Usually, he would draw the line at such an idea. He had done it once before, and as much fun as he had in the moment, it led to a lot of sleepless nights while he dreaded repercussions by the police. To his knowledge, nothing came of it. Of course, the incident took place four states away, but all the same, he figured some lines were not meant to be crossed.

But having a gun fired at him made him reconsider.

"Maybe," he replied.

"There's two other people with them now," Joe said.

"What? Mr. 'Let's all get along' and his wife?" Redge replied. "Yeah, I'm sure they'll cause us grief."

"I know, but if we're gonna get even, it would be more enjoyable if we regrouped with Freddy and the rest of the gang."

Redge thought about it. Joe was technically correct. To get even with those wannabe outdoorspeople, it would be better to have numbers on their side. But knowing Freddy, he would take charge of the whole thing—even going as far as making sure he was the first to help himself to Ms. Red Highlights.

"Yeah, fine," he said. "You wanna go link up with them?"

Joe nodded. "I'm not sure how soon we'll get back. I think they're cooking up some meth over by the usual spot."

"Yeah, whatever," Redge said. "Just get it done. I'll wait here with Hunter. I want to be able to keep an eye on those shitheads in case they change locations."

Knowing it was best not to argue with the brother of their gang leader, Joe nodded in agreement and went for his bike. He mounted up, revved the engine, then took off to the north.

After his friend vanished into the distance, Redge looked at his knife, then lined up with the tree he had been taking his anger out on. Its trunk was marked by a large number of shallow stab wounds from his insignificant blade, the ground behind it showing small grooves from the occasions in which he missed.

Picturing that guy in the tank top, Redge tossed the knife. It skidded over on the left side, hitting the ground.

Hunter chuckled, then tried to mask it as just him clearing his sinuses after receiving a deathly look from Redge.

"Something funny?"

"No, not at all," Hunter said. He was digging into his pocket for his stash. "Just, you know…" He held it out in a friendly offering. "Want any?"

"Not now," Redge said. "Later… at the appropriate time."

He picked his knife up and took position for another throw.

The knife flung from his fingers, wheeling once before driving its tip a couple of millimeters into the tree.

Redge pumped his fist, taking joy at the accuracy of his throw. Meanwhile, Hunter snorted again, and it was not from taking in a bump of his product. Redge turned around, eyebrows slanted and brow furrowed.

"What?"

Hunter, once again, tried to play dumb.

"Nothing!"

"Speak freely," Redge barked.

Hunter flinched, the tone not exactly matching with the spoken words. He pointed at the knife in the tree.

"It's just that, um, I think it would be cooler if you got the blade deeper into the tree."

Redge looked at it and shrugged. "It's a tree. It's made of wood. Of course the stupid thing isn't gonna go far."

"Yeah, but come on. You throw like a girl. You put a little bit of wrist action in it, but that's it. If that was what's-his-name standing there, that same throw would give him a little flesh wound. Shit, I've had love bites that were worse than what that'd inflict. You need to put real power into the throw." Hunter laughed, his drug eliminating any worry of offending Redge. "But you won't, because every time you do more than a wrist-flick, you miss."

He tucked his head low and started laughing like an idiot.

Redge grimaced at him, contemplating using him as a human practice target. Doing so would not be wise, as Hunter had a couple of loyal buddies in the gang. Even though Freddy was the leader, they would quickly break away in retaliation of such an act.

Also, it was more satisfying to prove Hunter wrong.

"Alright. I'll show you how it's done." He marched to the tree and yanked his knife free. He went to his spot, took a breath, and envisioned his opponent in place of that tree.

Nothing pleased his sick mind more than the thought of that blade buried deep in that asshole's gut, and the reaction of the guy clutching himself while crying for help. Then there was the vision of his girl hollering at the taking down of her man, followed by more screams of what was to come next.

Fueled by this fantasy, Redge threw the knife with all his might.

It soared through the air, the tip of its blade heading east… passing the target by over a foot as it went several yards into the distance.

Hunter fell back against the stump he was leaning on, his face red with laughter.

"Oh, Redge!" He slapped his knee, unable to regain control. "You poor bastard! Maybe you'll want to come up with a different method of getting even with the guy."

"Hunter…" Redge raised a finger. "I'd recommend shutting your mouth."

Hunter was too drugged out to feel the heat from the threat. He reached into his back pocket and pulled out a large folding knife.

"Here. This has more weight than that little pig sticker you're using. Bigger blade too. This should do the trick for you. You know, provided you aim right. On that note, I'd suggest compensating by aiming a little more to the right."

Redge had a few remarks in store for the idiot, but he knew that rotted brain would only find them funny. It was better to just throw the blade and satisfy his own ego.

He snatched the knife out of Hunter's hand. The guy wasn't lying; it had plenty of weight to it. A good throw would drive that six-inch blade into the hide of a buffalo, let alone the camper.

Redge assumed his usual stance, extended the blade, and drew his arm back. He released the knife, deliberately aiming high, as his fantasy now entailed it going through his enemy's eye socket. He grinned feverishly in anticipation of a bullseye, then shrank as it went to the right of the trunk, twirling far into the woods.

Hunter slapped his knee and laughed. "There it goes!"

Redge turned, ready to give him a genuine beating, only to bounce on his heels after hearing a deep roaring sound from within the forest.

Hunter perked up. "Whoa! Sounds like you hit something, Redge. Maybe you're not as bad at this as I thought."

Redge moved near the target-practice tree. "What the hell was that?"

"Probably an elk."

"Elks don't make that sound, stupid."

Hunter shrugged. "A bear, then."

Both men went quiet as stomping footsteps came their way.

Redge, feeling the blood drain from his face, started moving for his bike. "I don't think that's a bear…"

From the shadows emerged a towering brown mass of fur. For a split-second, Redge did think it to be a grizzly. Then he saw its man-like shape and the simian structure of its face, minus the imperfections caused by what had to have been some sort of disease or fungal infection.

None of that affected the sheer terror inflicted by just the sight of this thing… this monster… this man-beast…

Bigfoot.

Redge inhaled. "Fuck me…"

The beast brought its hand to its left shoulder and yanked the folding knife free. Keeping it pinched between its massive thumb and index finger, it peeled its lips, exposing jagged, unevenly proportioned teeth.

Hunter looked at his stash. "Damn. I think I need to cut back on this shit."

The beast roared and came at them.

In the blink of an eye, all sense of aggression had fleeted from Redge's body. He turned around and made a run for his bike.

Heavy footstep closed in on him, stopping abruptly as the beast came across Hunter, who was still seated near the stump.

Only when it grabbed the guy by his neck did he realize it was not a figment of his meth-induced imagination.

Bigfoot, holding him like a poacher with a dead goose, approached the fat trunk of a tree, and shoved Hunter against it. His head disappeared into red mush droplets, the rest of him twitching under the large finger that held him.

Dropping the dead biker's corpse, Bigfoot strutted for the man who had pissed it off.

Redge put himself on his bike and started it up. "Come on, come on, come on…"

He caught a glimmer of light bouncing off a metal object sailing through the air.

SPLISH!

Redge's jaw hung open, his airway closed off. The creature's aim was on point, having driven the knife right through his neck, as though it had done it a million times before.

The curtains closed in on his vision, concluding the show that was his thirty-eight years of life.

Bigfoot watched with satisfaction as his corpse slumped against the handlebars of his ride. Growling in mockery of the dead human, it turned around and went about its business.

Since its escape, it was unsure whether it wanted to seek out and kill more humans, or avoid them and go back into hiding. The insignificant, but painful injury sustained by the knife throw put an end to that debate.

All humans were fair game, and Bigfoot would take immense pleasure from tearing every single one of them apart.

CHAPTER 6

Arsenio Vogler watched the security tape on his flatscreen, his breathing intensifying as he witnessed the man in black plant two bullets in his brother's chest. Even worse was the fact that Ennio did not die on the spot. He had to suffer the excruciating sensation of having all the air driven out of his lungs first. Next, the killer ended his life with a third round to the head, before going to war with the fools who passed for Ennio's security force.

A bunch of cowards, they were. Cowardly and incompetent. They were so used to interacting with Trenton Loar that it did not occur to them that he posed a threat to Ennio. If there was any consolation, it was the fact many of them were now too dead to repeat their failure.

Arsenio would see an increase in his wealth as a result of this. With his brother dead, he would inherit his operations, territories, contacts, and resources. But that did not mean he was happy.

Far from it.

He wanted the man responsible for this atrocity dead. Not just him, but the traitors who helped him with the escape. It was evident that Trenton had help, not just in getting through the gates, but in planning the execution. It was too early yet to examine all of the surviving security footage, especially with many of the computers getting damaged from the explosions. With a little luck, they would all still be traveling together.

Standing in front of his desk was a man named Bennett. He was a stone-faced individual, more than happy to put an end to anyone's life, so long as the price was right. Even in this meeting, he was ready to go to war. He wore pistols on each thigh, had fingerless gloves on both hands, and bore the many marks from hazards on the field.

Arsenio lit a cigar and offered one to Bennett, who accepted.

"You know this man, Trenton Loar?"

Bennett puffed on his stogie and nodded. "We worked together on a couple of assignments."

"I see." Arsenio took a long draw, filling the office with tobacco smoke. "I'd ask if he's as good as my brother used to say he was, but given the body count he left behind, I think I have my answer."

"Heh!" Bennett tried not to chuckle too obnoxiously, considering the nature of this meeting. "With all due respect to your brother, I tried to warn him about his private security. Those guys weren't terrible, but they had gotten too rusty. They were used to nothing ever happening, and Trenton was counting on that. Plus, he knew he could sneak a pistol in to get the initial job done, then access Ennio's private weapons stash to break free."

"Your point?" Arsenio said, spewing smoke.

"It was a dangerous job, but Trenton was a queen going up against pawns in a chess game. Even with numbers on their side, it was a piece of cake for him." He took a nice long draw of his cigar before plucking it from his mouth. "So, yes, Trenton Loar is very good. Maybe even the best." A smile followed the statement. "Next to me."

Arsenio gave another look at the security footage. "I want him dead. Honestly, I'm not one of those guys who needs to drag it out with a blowtorch, pliers, or whatever else you see in the movies. All I want, prior to him going lights out, is for Trenton Loar to know killing Ennio Vogler was a mistake, and that his brother was the one to take him down." He held his hand out. "With you as my weapon, of course."

Bennett smiled. He was not one with an ego to bruise. Like many in his trade, he only cared about getting paid on time.

"I took the liberty of having my own guys run an inventory of missing items from your brother's mansion," he said.

Arsenio sat up, intrigued. "Yes?"

"As we both know, Trenton had help. It was a pretty well-put-together plan overall. With all the mangled bodies and the fire that swept through the place after the explosion, we haven't even identified all the fatalities. But!" He snapped his fingers, ordering his team into the office. Arsenio nodded at the door guard, confirming their right to enter.

Four men and one woman, all hard-nose killers, stepped inside. There was Gates, Donner, Cuomo, Wally, and Jackson. Naturally, Arsenio found himself looking at Jackson, particularly her tone body structure. A powerful man, Arsenio was used to having any woman he wanted. For once, he saw one who he would probably not retaliate if he heard the word 'no', for she looked like she could kill him a hundred different ways with her bare hands.

It was a ferocity carried by the other four team members. Bennett chose well when assembling his team. They were no nonsense people who were not here to play. They just wanted to know which way to point their guns.

The one named Donner placed a tan folder on Arsenio's desk. The crime boss opened it up and looked at a photo of a burnt room. In the center of the image was a large lockbox with its door open. The box itself showed some signs of damage, but overall, appeared intact.

He understood the meaning of this photo. It had been opened prior to the firefight, its contents taken.

"What did Ennio have in there?"

"Based on what the surviving staff in charge of that area have told us: diamonds," Bennett answered.

"Hmm." Arsenio flaked some of the ash off his cigar. "I didn't think Trenton was a petty thief."

"He's not." Bennett grinned widely while enjoying his smoke. "But one of the idiots he hired is. Those diamonds were not meant to be moved. One of the accomplices thought they could take the diamonds without anyone noticing, or caring. But he made a critical error; something Trenton did not consider."

Jackson put a tablet on the desk. On its screen was a map with a small red light blinking in some forest region several miles away.

"Ennio had a tracker on one of the diamonds?"

"Invented by yours truly," Bennett said proudly. "The tracker is designed to actually look like one of the diamonds. You'd need one of those microscope thingies to tell the difference. In our case, we have a little scanner to identify it should Ennio have decided he was ready to sell them off."

Arsenio did the math in his head. Trenton had chosen poorly when it came to one of the people helping him.

"If they're traveling together, you'll find the bastard," he said. "And if they separated, you can cut the traitorous shit to pieces until he gives you Trenton's location."

"That's the plan," Bennett said.

Arsenio opened a briefcase with a hell of a lot of cash inside. "Consider that a down payment. To get the rest, I want Trenton's body. Or, at least his head."

Bennett examined the money, then shut the briefcase.

"Consider it done."

Without saying another word, he and his team turned around and exited the office. It was time to hunt.

CHAPTER 7

As evening passed over Wiregrass Forest, the natural sounds of the nocturnal activity began its usual melody. In the distance, frogs and crickets sang their tunes, while the buzzing of flies and mosquitos droned overhead. Every so often, a loon made its call, at once eerie and beautiful, as was the call from its mate.

A campfire danced between the two tents. Heather and Betty talked about annoying people from the firm, getting opinions out of their systems that they could not share in the office.

"I swear!" Betty exclaimed, going on about her boss. "Not two minutes after he asks me to check the client's schedule, he tells me to immediately book a dinner with them at the Spaghetti Warehouse for Tuesday afternoon at five. I'm like, 'okay, but I don't know if they'll be free.' Another two minutes go by, and he comes back, latte in hand, asking if they have gluten-free noodles."

"As if you work in the kitchen," Heather said with a laugh.

"Right?"

On the other side of the fire, Bradford was watching his wife, totally losing track of what his conversation partner, Shawn, was talking about.

"…So, what do you think I should do?"

Bradford cringed. It was the dreaded question everyone in his situation desperately hoped to avoid.

Shit. What was he talking about? There was something about managing staff, something about going to the gym... more stuff about staff... Where does he work again?

"That's a good question," he replied. "Has, uh, Betty given you any ideas?" He watched the smoked sausage on the end of his stick, gradually warming up over the flames, hoping Shawn's response would give some clues to what he was talking about.

"Um..." Shawn laughed anxiously. "Why would she give me ideas on the surprise trip she doesn't know about?"

"Oh, right. Duh!" Bradford held his head down, embarrassed. At least he now understood the topic. "If I were her, I'd want you to take me to Vegas."

Shawn's body language only grew more awkward.

"She'd kill me. Because her father had a gambling addiction, remember?"

"Oh, right! Sorry, I got your story mixed up with..." He tried to dream up a name, "...Jerome at my work. He's been talking about Vegas all the time. I'm like, just go, man. Stop filling my ear with it."

The women perked up.

"What's this crap about Vegas?" Betty said.

"Oh, just swapping work stories," Bradford replied.

Heather looked away, deep in thought. "I went to your company's Christmas party last year. I don't remember anyone named Jerome."

Bradford tightened his lips and wrinkled every inch of skin on his face with tension. *Not helping!*

"Oh, my God!" Betty stood up, eyes on Shawn. "You're planning a trip to Vegas, aren't you?"

Shawn put his hands up, dropping his smore. "No, no, no, babe!"

She pointed a finger. "I warned you after you went with your brother last year, if you want to stay married to me, you'll stay far away from any casino. My dad blew away every dime he ever saved up all in the pursuit of winning a few bucks."

"Babe, no!" Shawn cried. "I promise, I'm not going to Vegas."

"Oh, really?" Betty said. "Then why was Bradford saying your story was like Jerome's, complaining nonstop about how he wanted to gamble? You talking shit about me over there? Just like I caught you doing with your brother a few months back? Yeah, I overheard that."

Shawn shook his head. "Sweetie, no! I was asking his advice about planning—Betty!" She stomped away, quickly distancing herself from the orange glow of the campfire. Shawn went after her, his voice getting more pathetic the farther they went.

After seeing the look Heather was giving him, Bradford was tempted to run off as well.

"You're pretty!" he said in an upbeat tone.

"What did you do?" she said.

"I didn't do anything!"

She tilted her head in the direction of the arguing couple. "Clearly."

Bradford moaned as though in physical torment. "He was going on, and on, and on, and on. I phased him out after a while."

"Right," she said. "That's why you compared his situation to Jerome's. Who is Jerome, by the way?"

"There's no Jerome!" Bradford put his smoked sausage on his plate and began attacking it with a fork and knife. It was the only acceptable target to take out his frustration. "I made it up after I got his story confused. I had tuned him out, then got blind-sighted by the usual 'what do you think' question. What was I supposed to say? 'Sorry dude, I wasn't listening to a word you said'?"

Heather cracked a grin. "Maybe not phrased like that." She started working on her own dinner. "What had you so distracted that you literally did not hear a word he said?"

"Well…" Bradford felt his heart flutter. The nice thing about what he was about to say was it was the truth. "I was thinking about you."

Heather laughed. "Oh really?"

"Really!"

"That's cute," she said. "Okay, now tell me the truth. What was on your mind?"

Bradford cocked his head back, that giddy feeling quickly fleeting. "No, that really was it."

"Yeah, I've heard that one before. You always think that's gonna get you out of trouble."

He stabbed his sausage. "First of all, I didn't do anything wrong. Secondly, *yes*, I was thinking about you. You're… I don't know. You're looking extra good tonight. Makes me think about all the good times we've had."

"Oh, of course you'd be thinking about sex," she muttered.

"No, I wasn't thinking about sex!" He broke eye contact and cleared his throat. "Okay, maybe a little bit, but I was thinking about us in general. I love you."

"Is that right?" she quipped, still not believing him.

"Yes, it is."

"That's cute." She stood up with her food on her paper plate. "Alrighty then, don't tell me." With her smoked sausage tucked into a bun, she walked into the woods to check on Shawn and Betty.

Bradford sat alone, his dinner sliced into countless pieces, humiliated and bothered by his wife's lack of confidence in his passion for her.

Now, more than ever, he missed his bed. At least at home, he was able to numb himself with the daily routine. But this was vacation, where he was supposed to feel better than ever. Every flaw in his personal life seemed to have a huge spotlight on it, even if he was the only one who noticed.

He tossed his plate and its contents into the fire. At least something out here was burning hot, because it wasn't the connection between him and Heather.

There were three more days planned for camping in Wiregrass Forest. Usually, three days went away in the blink of an eye for Bradford. Out here, it felt like an eternity, and it was only the first night.

He sighed.

Look on the bright side, Brad; it's not like this trip can get much worse. Really, what else could happen?

CHAPTER 8

The plan seemed to be working so far. To the rest of the world, they were a bunch of ordinary campers making their way through Wiregrass Forest. Nobody had reason to believe the five people were those responsible for the death of Ennio Vogler and his little empire.

Five miles from the mansion, they dumped their vehicles into a river and got together in a rusty SUV. On the outside, it was ratty looking, but inside it was practically new.

It was a vehicle that had been purchased by a friend of Matt Bing two days ago and gifted to him, with no paper trail to be traced by associates of their late employer. Not only that, but Trenton Loar was heading for one area nobody would consider looking for him.

That was where Billy Howard came into play. In addition to wanting to stick it to Ennio Vogler for crappy treatment over the last few years, he was interested in the cash payment Trenton Loar was offering.

Billy knew a precise, albeit unconventional route to get to their safehouse. Years back, his grandmother died and left a small cabin to his sister in Wyoming. Fortunately for Billy, his sister gave him the key and told him he could use it whenever he wanted. It was a long drive and they needed to avoid places where they would be seen, even publicly. Given the nature of their crime, those who would retaliate would not worry about appearances. The five of them would be gunned down in broad daylight if that's what it took to avenge Ennio Vogler.

It was for this very reason they chose to stop for the night and make camp. With the trails so narrow and the forest thick, it was not wise to drive through the aera at night. Doing so would only gain attention.

Trenton set up a small campfire. Like a cowboy in the Old West, he set up a small pot above its center, roasting some canned goods.

Jerry Griffith and Carl Malley sat together. The youngest of the band of criminals, they were still exhilarated by what they had accomplished.

"You see how that place went up?" Jerry asked his pal.

"Yes, we all saw it," Trenton said before Carl could answer. He was sick of enduring their back and forth. Having served as cooks for Ennio, they rarely saw any kind of real action. Most of their time was spent in the basement of a laundry cleaning facility, cooking up Ennio's product, often joking about being the real-life *Walter White* and *Jesse Pinkman*. To nobody's surprise, they were both a little closer to the latter character in terms of personality, especially as portrayed in the first season of the show, and their product was nowhere near the quality of the blue stuff.

"I can't believe those guys didn't check the C4 Trenton made us plant at the gate," Carl laughed.

"Man, it was like we were playing *Call of Duty*, except better!"

Trenton stirred the pot, thinking to himself, *I can shoot these morons right now, and nobody would know. Or care.*

"How did you do that, anyway?" Billy Howard asked.

"There's a little vent that comes up near the gate," Jerry said. "We sometimes do a little cooking under the mansion when the laundry place is undergoing cleaning. We just told them we were checking it to make sure the filtration system was working properly. They didn't think anything of it."

"Mind keeping it down?" Trenton hissed. "Don't forget, we're supposed to be keeping a low profile."

Billy smoked his joint and held his arms out at the blackness surrounding their camp. "There's nobody here."

"That you can see," Trenton replied. "Last thing we need is for some hiker to overhear you guys talking about blowing up property, killing people, and cooking your crappy meth. Our ride may go unnoticed by associates of Ennio, but it'll stand out like a sore thumb to anyone getting a description of us."

"True," Matt Bing said. He rubbed his hand over his face. "I should probably give myself a shave and a haircut. Make myself less recognizable."

"Right," Billy said. "They'll see all the cuts and bumps on your face and be totally fooled." He stood up, sipping on a mug of very low-quality coffee. "You sure we can't pitch a tent, Trenton?"

Carl sniggered. "You missed an opportunity there."

"Huh?"

Jerry joined his fellow cook in laughter. "Should've shortened his name to Trent. Get it? Tent, Trent?"

The two idiots laughed and smoked their joints.

Trenton glared at them, hating that he had no better choices for help in his recent betrayal of Ennio. Most people under the guy's thumb were totally loyal. Those who weren't were too scared of the repercussions. Only these four nitwits were the only rats he could put to use against his target.

He exhaled. The drive to Wyoming would be long. Then there was the fact he would be sharing a cabin with them for a month or two. Even worse, he was *paying* them. A substantial sum, too.

"I gotta take a shit," Carl said. He got up and walked away.

"Was that really worth announcing?" Billy asked.

Trenton appreciated that question. Of the four accomplices, he seemed to have the most sense.

Matt got up and walked to the truck. "Anyone up for some smores?"

"No." Trenton's voice was cold and harsh.

"Geesh." Matt opened the trunk. "Sorry I asked."

Trenton stirred the pot once more. The 'hobo soup' as he called it, was just about ready.

"Help yourselves," he said to the others sitting around the fire. He gestured at some paper bowls and plastic silverware on a big rock they used for a table. "Make sure you put the trash in a garbage bag when you're done." He got up to walk to where he had placed his sleeping bag, only to stop and do a double-take at something he saw in the grass near Jerry.

It was black and as flexible as paper, though smoother.

Trenton marched over to it and picked up the Hershey bar wrapper, nearly shoving it in Jerry's face.

"The hell is this?"

Jerry leaned away. "Um, chocolate?"

"What's it doing out here?" Trenton growled.

Jerry made a very worried laugh, suddenly remembering that this was a guy who had massacred a small army single handedly. And now he was pissed at *him*.

"I didn't think anything of it," he said. "We're technically camping. I thought it would make for a nice snack around the fire. I mean, didn't you hear Matt saying something about offering smores?"

Trenton crunched the wrapper in his fist. "This stuff attracts bears, idiot. We've got enough trouble on our hands. Last thing we need is to wake up to one of those things digging through our camp."

Jerry looked at the pot. "But they won't smell the stew?"

"They tend not to eat boiling hot stuff," Trenton said. He turned away, stuffing the wrapper in the garbage bag. "Get rid of any more sweets you may have. Your idiot friend doesn't have any, does he?"

Jerry shrugged. "I don't think so."

"Good." Trenton was not convinced by the answer, but he chose to be satisfied with it. After all, he was not interested in tracking Carl down while he was taking a dump.

He took the bag to the vehicle to best mask the scent of the trash inside. At the trunk, Matt was ruffling through some items, uncovering a large briefcase. Trenton had seen it during the switching of vehicles and didn't ask questions, believing it to be personal belongings.

It was open, exposing the merchandise inside.

"What the hell is that?" Trenton said in a sharp whisper.

Matt shut the briefcase. "Nothing."

"The hell do you mean, 'nothing'?" He grabbed the briefcase and lifted it wide open. Trenton was often not one to be speechless, but this moment was a strong exception.

There had to be fifty million dollars' worth of diamonds in the case.

"Where'd you get these?"

Matt shifted, not wanting to give the answer. "Oh, you know, you shop around, sometimes you find a good deal on some stuff…" The fiery glare from the assassin made him cut to the chase. "Alright, fine. I had helped Ennio pick these up. Don't ask me how he got 'em, because I don't know. What I do know is there's a guy in Vancouver who's willing to pay sixty-mil for them."

Trenton kept his expression blank to conceal his interest. "Sixty million?"

"Yes," Matt said. "Listen, I knew you were going to off Ennio, so I figured why let these diamonds get claimed by someone else? I was the only one who knew about them other than Ennio and some other security contractor he worked with… actually, I thought it was you."

"No, it wasn't me," Trenton said. He began sorting through the entire briefcase, checking every diamond as well as the case itself.

Matt watched in silence for the first couple of minutes before finally asking, "What are you looking for?"

"I'm making sure there's not a tracking device hidden in this thing," Trenton replied.

"There isn't," Matt said.

"Like you would know." Trenton continued searching, even checking the individual jewels themselves. From what he could see, there was no transmitter he recognized.

"Listen, I was gonna mention it to you anyway," Matt said. "Let's face it, I need a little bit of muscle while I make my deal. Otherwise, there's nothing to keep the buyer from just blowing my head off and taking the diamonds. I want my money, even if it's only half."

Trenton read between the lines. That word 'half' had specific meaning.

"You're splitting this with me?"

Matt glanced at the guys at the campfire, making sure they didn't overhear the conversation. "Yes."

Trenton cooled down. He could tell Matt was serious in his offer, which led him to reflect on his own career up to this point. He did well financially, but even with what he earned, his savings would only last him so long. One big issue was the cost of getting himself a new identity. Being the man who killed Ennio Vogler, he would never be trusted by any client ever again, not even the ones who benefitted from Ennio's death. It did not matter as to *why* Trenton killed him. In the end, he was a guy who betrayed his employer, therefore, nobody would take a risk by hiring him.

That reality meant two things: he was essentially retired, and what he had in cash would largely go to the man who would give him a whole new name and identity. Earlier, he was living the finale of *Scarface.* Today, he was living the final episodes of *Breaking Bad.* Unlike the lead character of that show, he actually planned to lay low indefinitely, using his funds to sustain himself to the end of time. The problem was the amount he would be left with was not practical.

Thirty million dollars changed all of that.

"You have that price locked in?" he asked Matt.

"Damn straight."

"What about money laundering?"

"I have a guy," Matt said. As a token of good faith, he pulled out a card for a lawyer with connections. This time, Trenton sniggered. His life seemed to be mirroring pop culture. "His rate is usually fifteen percent. I was able to talk him down to ten."

Trenton nodded. Ten was good. He could easily make twenty-seven million work.

"Is he aware you'll be hiding out of sight for a while?"

Matt nodded. "He is. He's good with it. After things cool down, I'll schedule a meeting with him. I just need you to be Mr. Badass and make sure we actually walk away with the money. Seeing how you handled yourself against all those guys at the mansion, I'm confident you'll do just fine."

Trenton gave one more good look at the diamonds. "Nobody else knows?" He tilted his head towards those around the campfire. *Them in particular?*

Matt shook his head.

Satisfied with that answer, he shut the briefcase and pushed it under Matt's other belongings.

"Don't lose track of it."

Matt smiled. "Don't have to tell me twice."

***

Carl Malley grunted, reminding himself of the importance of drinking water and laying off the donuts. Being out in the open did not make things any easier. Like most people, he preferred the seclusion of an enclosed space where he was probably not being watched from afar.

His small lantern was several feet away, next to his bag of goodies he had placed on a log. No way was he going to leave his chocolate bars with Jerry. The prick would stuff them all in the few minutes Carl would be away on business.

Or a few *hours*, based on the way things were going now.

"Ugh. Maybe some of Billy's crappy coffee might help move things along."

Snap!

He looked into the darkness, thinking one of his fellow fugitives were approaching, only to remember they were camping in the opposite direction of that sound.

A *thump* that was an obvious footstep rocked the ground in that same direction.

Carl started to sweat. He was in the worst predicament one could imagine, for things were not moving along, but were at a point where he could not simply pull his pants up and move away.

His only option was to try and get whatever or whoever was coming to go away.

"Um, sorry," he said. "This area's occupied. Mind giving a fella some privacy?"

He heard another footstep. Then another.

The rate of the sounds of motion were consistent with those of a person walking, though a little heavier.

Maybe it's some fat drunk guy.

"Eh-hem! Excuse me… you mind heading back the way you came? I'd appreciate it."

The sounds came closer.

Carl leaned forward and felt the small pocket pistol he had holstered around his sock. He hoped not to use it, but this visitor was starting to piss him off.

"Last chance!"

He heard a bush get uprooted and a large object, probably a broken branch, get knocked out of the way.

In the glow of the light, the visitor arrived.

Carl's heart skipped a beat. This 'guy' was fourteen feet tall and looked more like an ape than a person.

With enormous feet that connected to the earth with sounds of thunder, it moved towards his bag of goodies. It sniffed, picking up whiffs of his chocolate bars.

Standing above the small lantern, its orange eyes turned to him.

Carl gulped.

All of a sudden, his plumbing was in free flow.

"AGH!"

The beast lunged with both hands outstretched.

***

"What the hell?"

Trenton and everyone else listened to the screams coming out of the darkness. Right away, they transformed into a mix of chaos, comprised of rustling vegetation, grunts of pain, and roars.

Jerry and Billy stood up.

"The hell's going on?" the former asked.

"Shit, he probably encountered a bear," Billy said. "I thought you said he didn't take any snacks out there with him."

"I'm not his daddy!" Jerry snapped. "I'm not gonna tell him what he can and can't do!"

The shouting concluded with a high-pitched "EEEGH!"

Next came the thrashing of leaves and branches high in the canopy as something soared through the woods, straight for the camp. Like a meteor trailing smoke, the object came crashing down right in the campfire… except that 'smoke' was blood and intestines.

Jerry and Billy jumped back, looking at the severed torso of Carl Malley.

Matt stumbled backward and fell on his rear. "Holy…"

"What the hell did this?" Jerry said. "A bear?"

"Right, because bears rip people in half," Billy remarked.

"You have a better explanation?" Jerry shouted. "Because no man could've done this! Had to have been a grizzly. Unless you're gonna tell me Sasquatch is stomping around in these woods!"

Stomp! Stomp! Stomp!

Both men froze, watching the shape emerge from the darkness into the glow of the campfire, which was currently cooking Carl.

Its humanoid shape eliminated the possibility of it being a bear. Its immense size and strength eliminated the possibility of it being a man.

Whatever it was, it was deadly.

Stomping onto the campsite, the huge beast parted its jaws and roared its fury at the group.

"Jesus!" Billy went to step back, only to trip over one of the rocks and fall into the campfire. Feeling the blazing heat, he screamed.

The beast approached, going after Jerry.

The druggie turned around and attempted to make a run for it. The beast proved to be faster, seizing him by the waist and lifting him off the ground.

"Put me down! Put me down! Holy SHIT!"

The creature decided to fulfill his wishes.

Grabbing him by both ankles, it flung him downward, splattering him against the tough soil. With every bone in his upper body broken, Jerry twitched.

The creature turned around, his face cracking what appeared to be a smile at the sight of Jerry floundering in the campfire.

`He managed to roll out of it, the back of his shirt completely burnt away by the hot embers, revealing red flesh.

The beast went up to him and kicked him back in, sparking a fresh wave of kicking and screaming from Billy Howard. It put its heel down on him, preventing him from rolling away.

Pinned between the monster's heavy foot and fires as hot as hell itself, Billy could do nothing but squirm and wail.

"Christ alive!" Matt exclaimed. "What the hell is that?!"

For once in his life, Trenton was wishing the answer would be another *Breaking Bad, Scarface,* or other crime-drama pop culture reference. But the truth was way weirder.

This was Bigfoot!

"Let's get out of here!" he shouted.

They went for the front seats of their vehicle.

Noticing their movements, Bigfoot decided not to risk the remaining two humans escaping its wrath. It pressed down on Jerry, reducing his center mass to sizzling jelly.

Oddly enough, that did not kill him right away. For Bigfoot, that made the human's fate all the more satisfying.

Leaving the pancaked Jerry to roast, it charged at the SUV.

Matt screamed and threw himself to the right, faceplanting over Trenton's groin.

"Get off of me!" the assassin yelled.

BAM!

In a single crashing impact, the vehicle fishtailed, its driver's side partially caved in.

Matt yelped, his leg caught where the door had folded over the driver's seat.

"I'm caught!"

Trenton opened his door and jumped out.

The beast struck again, this time hitting the back half of the vehicle, producing a similar result. Fists hammered down hard on the ceiling, crunching it inward.

Trenton opened the trunk and pulled out his duffle bag, jumping back just in time to avoid Bigfoot's hammering fist.

He unzipped the bag, revealing the M16 he had taken from Ennio's mansion. Much to his disappointment, there were no grenades left. But there was a full magazine loaded, and he was ready to put it in full use.

Bigfoot hit the SUV with a right hook, knocking it on its side. Huffing and puffing like the big bad wolf himself, it walked around the vehicular wreckage and strutted towards the assassin.

Clenching his teeth, he shouldered the rifle and unleashed a steady stream of bullets into the beast.

Blood popped from its chest, forcing the monster backwards. Hollering in pain and fury, it turned around and retreated into the forest.

Trenton kept up the punishment, hitting the creature in the back in hopes of landing a lucky shot.

The magazine ran dry, forcing him to stop.

Silence consumed the campsite, ending with Matt's grunting as he attempted to dislodge the driver's side door.

He managed to kick it open and crawl out. Popping his head into the open like a mole, he glanced about.

"Where'd it go?"

Trenton pointed south.

Matt waited quietly, listening to the sounds of its retreat getting more and more distant. After a while, everything went completely silent.

"Fuck!" he gasped. He looked at the M16 in Trenton's hands. "You think it's dead?"

Trenton loaded a fresh magazine and made sure his sidearm had a round chambered.

"One can only hope."

Matt turned his eyes to the trail of destruction. "Was that what I think it was?"

"It appears so," Trenton said bluntly.

"I thought it was only a legend," Matt said. "Or a hoax. Some people say the famous pictures are actually of a guy in a suit."

"Well, if that's the case, that's the most convincing costume I've ever seen," Trenton said. He went to the vehicle and started picking out all of the supplies they could afford to carry.

Matt lifted himself out of the driver's seat. "What do we do now? No way are we going anywhere in this thing."

Trenton shook his head. "We're not staying here either."

"Wait, really?" Matt held his hand out to bring attention to the darkness of night consuming the forest. "You want to *walk?* In this? After what we've just been through?"

"You'd rather stay here?" Trenton said. "With that thing knowing where we're at?"

Matt bit his tongue. It was a fair enough point.

"So, that's it? We're just gonna walk?"

"And find someone who can give us a ride," Trenton added. He grabbed his two duffle bags. One was loaded with cash withdrawn from his accounts. The other held his assault rifle, some ammo, and some extra clothes. "Don't forget our special package."

"Oh!" Matt jogged for the back of the SUV. "Right!" He grabbed the briefcase and a backpack with some of his personal belongings.

Once his partner was ready, Trenton led the way.

The beast had gone south. In his mind, it was only logical to go north. Luckily, it was the direction they needed to go anyway.

With one hand resting on his sidearm, he stepped out of the light of the dying campfire, Matt Bing right behind him.

CHAPTER 9

Most mornings, Bradford woke up to the infuriating sounds of an alarm clock. On the weekends, it was to the antics of his three sons who suddenly became early birds on the few occasions he didn't have to drag their asses out of bed for school. As much as he was not looking forward to sleeping in the blistering summer heat without his air conditioning, he at least took joy in knowing there was nothing that would demand he leap out of bed.

Of course, that was what he *anticipated.*

Granted, what woke him up this morning was not something that required his attention, but it was impossible to ignore.

"You've got to be kidding me."

The passionate racket from the neighboring tent was without any decency or discretion. By the sound of it, Shawn and Betty may as well have been animals, grunting and gasping, even screaming out a couple of times, with no care who was listening.

He lay on his back, taking in the sounds, while slightly envying their marital passion. Credit where it was due, Shawn was doing a hell of a job over there.

In a way, Bradford was jealous. Shawn was ten years younger than him and didn't have the stress of parenthood weighing on his mind. But the unconscious part of Bradford's mind refused to take that into consideration.

Staring up at the tent ceiling, he cracked a smile.

Why complain when you can problem solve right here?

He rolled to his left and reached over to embrace his wife. What he got was a hollow sleeping bag.

Bradford pushed the dispassionate inanimate object away, then sat up. She was not in the tent.

Freeing himself from his own bag, he stepped outside, breathing a sigh of relief when he found his wife seated in a folding chair, noticeably a little far away from the camp.

She was deep into a book, with a pair of headphones on, of course.

Bradford approached. "Good morning." She didn't hear him. "Ah-hem! Good morning!"

She looked up and smiled. "Oh, hey! Good morning!"

"You okay?"

She looked at Shawn and Betty's tent and grimaced. "Technically, yes."

The sounds of passion reached a high-pitched conclusion from both members involved, winding down with heavy gasps and steadying breathing rates.

Heather sighed. "Lucky bitch."

Bradford looked at her. "Beg your pardon?"

"Hmm? Oh, nothing."

"No, I heard you," he said. He composed himself for a moment, not wanting this exchange to be overheard by their camping partners. "What did you mean by that? You mean you…wish *you* were in there, banging Shawn?"

Heather laughed. "Oh, hell no."

"What then?"

"Honey, relax!" she exclaimed. "I'm just…"

She was interrupted by the appearance of Shawn Menger, bursting from his tent in his birthday suit, his anatomy still winding down from the recent activity.

He stretched his arms out and took in the morning air with a satisfied, "Ahhh!"

"Um, 'morn'n, Shawn," Bradford said.

Shawn looked at them. "OH!" He covered himself up and backed into the tent.

Bradford and Heather stared in stunned silence.

"He actually forgot we were here," Heather said.

"I'd say you're correct," Bradford added. After another minute of quiet, he grabbed a folding chair and sat next to his wife. "Still think Betty's lucky?"

"That's not what I meant," Heather said.

"Yeah, I know I don't do it for you anymore," Bradford continued. "I don't have the nice hair, the abs, the charm. I try, but I guess it's only something for the young."

Heather shifted in her seat. "What are you talking about?"

"I…" He looked away. "Nothing."

"There's something," she said. She put a hand on his shoulder. "Sweetie, what is it?"

"Oh, it's stupid."

"Hey. You can tell me anything."

Bradford felt a warmth from those words. There was genuine affection in her voice. It was something he had not noticed in quite a while. At least, not that he picked up on.

"I can?"

"Absolutely."

"You'll think it's stupid."

Heather shook her head. "No way." Her hand rubbed his shoulder. "Go ahead, Brad. Spit it out. I'm listening."

Bradford tapped his hands against his knees while trying to articulate his concerns. Maybe this trip was turning out to be worthwhile. Finally, he was able to open up a true dialogue with Heather and clear the air.

"I was just thinking, you and—"

The tent fluttered open again. This time, it was Betty who stepped out in the open, with nothing but the sunlight covering her body. Like her husband, she stretched her arms and exclaimed with an audible "Ahhh!"

Bradford raised his eyebrows, his eyes by nature looking over her slim stomach and the perky features above.

"Whoa!"

Betty looked over at them. Just like her husband, she covered up and backed into the tent.

Bradford was frozen stiff in shock and slight arousal. "Are we in a movie?"

"I wish," Heather muttered. "That way we could yell 'cut' and have some people thrown off the set."

She stood up and began walking away.

Bradford continued staring at the tent, noticing his wife's absence after several moments.

"Oh, hey!" He chased after her. "What's wrong?"

"Nothing," she said in an obvious lie. "Sorry, just… frustrated at them. You were right. Inviting them was a dumb idea. I knew those two are hot and heavy for each other, but we're so insignificant to them, they actually forgot we're here."

"They might be drunk," Bradford said.

Heather stopped and faced him. "That makes it better?"

"M-maybe?" He tried to think of something better to say.

Back at the camp, the Mengers' tent opened up again. Shawn and Betty stepped out, this time wearing swim outfits.

"We're heading over to the lake," Shawn called to them, as if no awkwardness had occurred in the preceding moments.

"Wanna come?" Betty asked.

Heather forced a smile. "N-no thanks. I'm gonna make some coffee."

"Alright!" Betty said, waving. "Make it double extra strong!"

She and her husband got into their orange Dodge Journey and took off for the lake.

Bradford looked at his wife. "Double extra strong? As in, just extra strong? Or is it quadruple strong?"

Heather glared at him. "You seriously expect to make any sense of that?"

Bradford gave the question some thought, then shook his head.

"Nope."

Agreeing with that sentiment, Heather walked to the fireplace and picked up the coffee pot.

Bradford remained in place, his moment of opportunity stripped from him. Sure, he was alone with Heather, but the antics of her coworker had shifted the mood away from one that harbored a meaningful discussion.

***

Shawn splashed into the lake, popping up several yards out with a satisfied, "Ahh!"

Betty jumped in next, gasping as her body acclimated to the slight chill. She paddled out and joined her husband in six feet of water.

"Feels good, doesn't it?" he said.

"Oh, yeah!" She made several large strokes, stopping a couple of times to fix her bikini top. The lake was maybe five hundred yards wide where they were at. She went another twenty feet out, feeling the weeds touching the bottom of her feet.

Shawn remained where he was.

"What? You too scared to come farther out?" she said to him.

"Ha! Listen, I'm good at running and weight-lifting. But swimming isn't exactly my strong suit."

"Wuss!"

"Yeah, laugh all you want," he said. "But I'm staying here where I can touch the bottom."

"Suit yourself."

Betty backstroked, gradually moving to the middle of the lake.

Shawn shook his head. "I'm not going out there."

Betty, now seventy feet from shore, took a break and looked over at him. She held her hand out and waved with her finger, her white smile completing the message.

Shawn laughed. "No, I think I'm good."

Betty paddled with her feet, keeping her head and shoulders above water. Suggestively, she pulled down the straps of her bikini top.

"Still not coming?"

That got Shawn's attention.

"Eh…" He waded in his spot, unsure if he could get his mechanics working again. Though he wasn't sure he could get it going, especially with the strain of trying to keep his head above water, he also didn't want to say no. Something about that was sacrilege, not just to him, but to all men in general.

The only way to save face was to challenge her in return.

"I don't think you could handle me all the way out there."

"Oh, is that right?" she said.

"That's right," he replied. "I'd hate for you to drown."

"Uh-huh!" In protest, she began swimming farther.

Now, Shawn was getting nervous.

"Seriously, babe. You don't have a lifejacket. If something goes wrong…"

"Quit being such a pussycat!" she called to him.

Shawn jerked back as though physically struck by the words. "Damn!" He inched forward, tempted to chase her down. When he got to the point he had to stand on his tippy toes to keep from submerging, he stopped. Maybe it was his low body fat, but swimming was not on his list of talents. He could swim for a short distance, but after a while, he would sink like a brick. Somehow, Betty didn't suffer that same handicap. She was practically made for the water. And she didn't have any formal training either. There was no swim team she was a part of. Even if years had passed in which she did not see any body of water bigger than a bathtub, she was still able to swim as though she did it every day.

She was a speck in the middle of the lake now, waving at him.

"Very cute!" he called to her. "Hey, you mind coming back?"

"My gosh! It's so cute how worried you are," she shouted.

"Yeah, well, drowning is a real hazard."

"I suppose!" She started throwing her arms about, feigning a struggle. "Oh, no! I'm drowning. Wahhh!"

She flipped herself upside down, letting her legs stick up straight in the air.

Shawn groaned. "Not funny!" He knew she couldn't hear him.

Those legs kept straight up.

Shawn did not want to admit it, but he found it impressive that she was able to maintain that pose. It was like something out of a cartoon.

Betty wheeled herself to the side, splashing her legs down and bringing her head back up.

"Wow!" Shawn raised his hands and clapped. "That was really—"

"S-Shawn!" She started paddling back to him as though the devil was right behind her. "Help!"

His heart felt as though it would spring from his chest. It was a sound no man wanted to hear from his wife.

"What's wrong?"

"There's—AGH!"

She went under.

"Betty!" He moved as far as he could, halted only by his lack of swimming talent. The water where she was swirled. He could envision his wife fighting to get a breath of air, unable to fight against gravity.

With a splash, she popped up.

For a split-second, Shawn was relieved.

Then he heard her scream. He knew pain when he heard it, and Betty was in a world of pain.

She clawed at the water, trying to get away from the spot she was in. In spite of her motions, she went *backwards*. After a few yards, she whipped to the side.

Her upper body shook, her mouth extending in a way similar to one felt when punched in the stomach. Or, though he never experienced it himself, stabbed.

Blood spat from her lips.

Grunting, she was whipped left and right, the water around her turning red.

Another splash caught Shawn's eye. It was several yards to the right of Betty, caused by a rigid fan-shaped object. Farther beyond it, another object breached the water. It was a dark green color and appeared rubbery in texture.

Betty went into a spin, the momentum stretching her arms to the side. With one final yelp, she went flying, her upper torso skipping over the water, flinging guts from her detached waist.

Shawn was lightheaded, unable to take his eyes off what he had just witnessed.

In doing so, he failed to take notice of the serpentine shape coursing through the water's surface, its bullet-shaped head aimed right at him. Once it closed within ten feet, he snapped out of his trance.

"Oh, fu—"

The beast, snake-like in its form, and with jaws rivaling the ferocity of a piranha, coiled its body, then launched itself at him.

Shawn was tackled into the water. Unlike his wife, who was ravaged on the lake's surface, he was pinned to the lakebed, his screams muffled by the silt and water while rows of pointed teeth shredded everything below his shoulders.

CHAPTER 10

Bradford emerged from his tent, having freshly dressed himself in relaxed-fit jeans and a white t-shirt. Heather was sipping coffee near the fire, at peace by the looks of it. She deserved it, after seeing more than she cared for of their camping buddies.

"Got any more of that coffee?" he asked.

She nodded and pulled another cup from her bag. "Here."

Bradford sensed trouble in her voice. Worse; humiliation.

"Are you okay?"

"Yeah, I'm fine." She sighed. "Maybe we should've gone to the casino. Could've gambled a little bit, pigged out on some buffets, drank a bunch of wine and margaritas, and remained blind to all of our issues."

"Hey, it's not too late to pack up and…" Bradford paused, that last part of her sentence sinking in. "Wait, our issues?"

"I saw the way you were looking at Betty," she said.

Bradford felt as though he swallowed his tongue.

"Whoa, whoa, whoa!" He had his hands out, literally trying to keep his balance. "Yeah, I *saw*. How could I have not?"

"No, that's not what I meant," Heather said. She exhaled sharply, failing to find the appropriate choice of words. "Sorry, that came out wrong. Yeah, those two are nuts with no sense of boundaries. Had I known that… eh, who cares?"

"I care," Bradford took a seat next to her. "About what's bothering you, that is."

"I'm worried about what's bothering *you*," she replied. "You've been acting strange lately."

"So have you."

"Not as much as you."

"I—" Bradford stammered. "Okay, we're talking in circles. Let's get to it. Should you go first, or should I? You know what? I'll just go. I've been trying to figure out the best way to put this." He played with a twig while articulating his thoughts.

Heather put a hand to her mouth. "Oh, God. You had an affair, didn't you?"

"What? No!" The words came out as half-laugh, half-croak. "No way would any woman want me anyway." He tossed the twig into the fire and decided to cut to the chase. Yeah, it would sound stupid, but not as much as beating around the bush. "Lately, it feels like you and I—"

He and his wife stood up at the sound of several motorcycles rolling into camp. Several hooligans, dressed in sleeveless shirts and dirty jeans, whooped and hollered. Many of them whipped chains over their heads like ancient natives about to launch an assault against unwanted explorers.

"There, Freddy! Those are the people!" one of the guys said.

"Just these two?" the leader named Freddy called from somewhere in the ring of bikes tearing through the camp. "I'm waiting on an answer, Joe! Are there any others?"

Bradford and Heather caught a glimpse of the one named Joe, instantly recognizing him as one of the three bikers getting testy with Shwan yesterday.

One of the bikes pulled up near the fireplace. The man on its seat had black hair combed backward, dark tan skin covering toned muscles, aviator sunglasses over his eyes, and an angry scowl on his face.

Freddy stepped off the bike and squared up with the nervous couple.

Bradford and Heather went to back away, only to find themselves boxed in by three of the other bikers.

"Hey, listen," Bradford said. "If you guys want your spot back, we were honestly thinking of leaving. Turns out, camping just isn't our cup of tea anymore."

A punch to the jaw knocked him to the ground.

"Stop!" Heather yelled. "What do you want?"

Freddy lowered his glasses. "You gonna act like you don't know?"

"Don't know what?" Bradford asked. He rolled to his hands and knees, touching his jaw.

Freddy kicked him in the stomach, putting him on his back once more.

"Don't talk to me like I'm stupid." He stomped on Bradford's stomach. "You killed my brother. Put a knife through his neck."

"Hunter too!" Joe said. "Only a true demon would do what you all did to him."

"What are you talking about?" Heather cried. "We haven't left this camp since we arrived."

"Where are your friends?" Freddy said.

"They didn't do anything either," Bradford said.

Freddy stomped once more. "Like I'm gonna believe that nonsense." He reached into his back pocket and pulled out a large folding knife. "I pulled this from my brother's throat." He held it close to Heather's neck.

In spite of the intense fear, she refused to leave Bradford's side.

"Brave woman," the biker leader continued. "Let's see how much she's willing to suffer before you tell me the truth…"

***

After ten hours of nonstop hiking, and listening to Matt Bing complaining about his aching feet, Trenton believed there was light at the end of the tunnel. All night long, he had hoped to find another camp and bum a ride to the nearest town. At last, he could hear voices.

He had no intention of mentioning the Bigfoot encounter. Every time he rehearsed it in his head, it sounded crazier and dumber. Explaining it to a stranger would definitely cost him a trip out of this forest.

As they neared the camp, there was a sound of motorcycle engines, operated by very unfriendly people.

Trenton and Matt found some bushes to crouch by and observe the altercation taking place. There were ten bikers surrounding two average-looking people. The leader, whose name was Freddy, brandished a knife and began threatening the woman, referred to by her husband as Heather. During the mix of exchanges, Trenton managed to overhear her refer to him by the name Bradford.

The rest, he did not care about. These self-proclaimed tough guys were a hindrance to his final goal.

"Not a friendly group of fellas," Matt whispered.

"Nope." Trenton looked at the camp. There was one vehicle parked near the tents.

"What's the plan?" Matt asked. "Should we wait it out? These guys might move on after they finish cutting up the guy and his lady. Then we can just take their car and get out of here."

Trenton shook his head. "No."

"Wait…" Matt looked at him. "You're not thinking of stepping in, are you? Since when did you grow a conscience?"

"I couldn't care less about them," Trenton said. "But I'm not thrilled about the idea of driving a stolen car, especially if its owners have recently been butchered in the woods. That's a good way of getting unwanted attention, not to mention false murder charges."

"So, what then?" Matt counted the hostiles. "There's ten of them."

"See any guns?"

"No. Don't think so."

"Good." Trenton checked his ankle holster in the event he may need it. "Then the odds are even."

There was no need to make a grand announcement or attempt to negotiate peace. Guys like Freddy's gang only responded to violence. Once faced with a superior threat, they backed down.

He emerged from hiding and dashed into the campsite. One of the bikers closest to him turned around, a chain-wrapped fist pulled back. Trenton struck first, plowing a fist across his jaw and knocking him to the ground.

Now in the middle of the crowd, he went to work dispatching the gang.

A chop to the throat dropped one of them to his knees. A kick to the chest sent another one tumbling backward, his head clunking against a tree trunk.

Freddy moved his knife from Heather's neck to combat the new threat.

Bradford lifted his foot, kicking the gang leader in the groin. Freddy stumbled backward, doubling over from the crushing pain. Bradford pushed himself up. With another kick, he separated the knife from Freddy's hand, then landed a fist to his nose.

"Look out!" Heather shouted, pointing behind him.

Bradford turned around, gasping as he saw one of the bikers coming at him with a tire iron.

Trenton stopped the attack short, intercepting the assailant and twisting his arm around his back. With multiple other enemies closing in, he spun the biker a hundred-eighty degrees, successfully using him as a human shield against a slashing chain.

"Oh, shit!" the biker said, watching his friend take the lash straight to the face. It was a phrase that was immediately repeated, albeit in a long, drawn-out groan, after Trenton cracked a rib with a powerful kick.

An elbow to the face put another one to the dirt.

Near the campfire, Freddy approached Bradford, intent on exacting revenge. The camper, still clutching his stomach where he had been repeatedly stomped, had to think fast.

He dove near the campfire, grabbing the coffee pot Heather had brewed, then whipped its boiling-hot contents onto Freddy's groin.

The seemingly tough-as-nails gang leader cried out in a voice so high-pitched, Bradford wasn't even sure it was his at first. Freddy, grasping his manhood, stepped backward.

Bradford moved in on him, his face red. An uppercut to the chin put Freddy on the ground.

The bike leader kicked his feet, scooting himself back. "I'll kill you! You won't get away with what you and your friends did to Redge."

"For the last time," Bradford said, "I didn't do anything! If he's dead, you should get the police."

"Too late for that," Trenton said. He had another one of the bikers locked in a grip. With a little bit of force, he put the guy's face against a tree, dropping him. "Ya'll fight like a bunch of schoolgirls. You'd think for people who live in the outdoors, you'd be in better shape."

Freddy picked himself up. "We're not done yet."

"No, I think we are," Trenton said. He reached near his ankle and drew his pistol.

Seeing its muzzle in front of his face, Freddy went quiet. Having gotten the message loud and clear, he and his men slowly retreated to their motorcycles.

Trenton kept the gun aimed at the bike leader, finger on the trigger, ready to make good on his unspoken threat.

Freddy mounted his ride and waited for his followers to do the same. A bunch of engines came alive at once.

He gave one last look to Trenton and Bradford.

You really stepped in it now.

Off he went, his followers trailing behind him.

Trenton kept the weapon fixed on the son of a bitch right up to the moment he was out of sight. Holstering the weapon, he waved in Matt's direction.

"Get out here, ya sissy."

"Whoa!" Matt came sprinting into camp. "That was a damn good fight!"

Heather hugged Bradford. "You okay?"

"Yeah, I'm good." He gave her a quick kiss, then approached Trenton. "Hey, thanks for the help."

Trenton shook his hand. "What can I say? I hate bullies."

"I guess so, seeing how well you took them on," Bradford said. As he caught his breath, he noticed the large duffle bags and briefcase their new visitors were carrying. "You guys okay? Pardon me for being nosey, but that doesn't look like a conventional hiking setup."

"It's not," Trenton said.

"Yeah, we originally had a set of wheels," Matt said. "We were passing through, when we had a bit of a… unfortunate encounter."

"They attacked you?"

Matt bit his lip. "Mmmm… well…"

"Yes," Trenton said. "They wrecked our truck and left us stranded. I was hoping you would be able to give us a ride out of here. I know it's inconvenient, given the distance and all…"

"Oh, heck, not at all," Heather said enthusiastically. "We'll be glad to get you out of here. Give us a minute to get our act together. We'll take down our tent and load up."

"Yeah, we're not too eager to stay out here, knowing those psychos might return," Bradford said.

"Excellent," Trenton said. "We greatly appreciate it."

"Before we take off, we need to make a slight detour," Heather said.

Trenton lifted his chin, trying his best not to look disappointed. "Oh?"

"There's another married couple out here with us. They're taking a swim in the lake," Bradford explained. "We need to warn them."

"On that note…" Heather went into the second tent, then came back out with a forty-caliber pistol. "I'm not thrilled with the idea of leaving this unattended, especially with those assholes nearby."

"Good thinking," Bradford said. "You hang on to it. You remember how to shoot, right?"

"It's been a hell of a while, but I think I got the gist," she quipped.

"Eh-hem!" Matt audibly cleared his throat. "Not to be a pain in the ass, but I'd like to get moving right away. I really don't want to stay out here a minute longer than I have to. Not with that thing—*gang* out there."

Bradford and Heather gathered their things and loaded up their truck.

"Relax," she said. "We're the ones with the guns. I think we can handle anything that comes at us."

Matt made a sound that could pass for either a laugh or a cry.

"Yeah…"

CHAPTER 12

The next few minutes were spent in silence while they followed the trail taken by Shawn and Betty. The tire tracks from their Dodge Journey were fresh, with no signs of motorcycle bandits having come this way.

Their new friends, Trenton and Matt, sat in the back, the former cradling his briefcase as though it was a newborn child. Bradford glimpsed at the man in his rearview mirror, finding their presence and behavior somewhat odd. The Trenton guy was a hell of a fighter. It was more than someone who attended a martial arts school once or twice a week. He was adept in close quarters combat, even against multiple foes. Had it not been for the ankle holster, Bradford would have simply chalked it up as him just being really good. But something about the guy screamed something much darker. Military, maybe. Black ops. Assassin.

It was movie-type stuff, nothing he ever expected to contemplate in real life. But here he was, contemplating it.

For now, all he cared for was to inform Shawn and Betty of the situation and make sure they got out of these woods. After that, they would be out of here.

As he drove, Bradford felt his wife's eyes on him. Her hand was on his thigh, occasionally squeezing his free hand.

He smiled. It was definitely a friendly gesture; a certain gesture he hadn't noticed in a good long while.

"What?" he said in a playful tone.

"Nothing," she said.

That was an obvious lie, and it was all part of the game.

"What?" he repeated.

Heather looked away like a shy high school student talking to her crush—a nice reminder of their life when they first met.

"Just… you kicked ass back there. I…" She closed her eyes and giggled. "I hope this doesn't come off as mean, but I didn't think you had it in you. But you did, and you sent that big, tough biker packing."

Bradford smiled, doing his best to play it cool.

"I'd like to take all the credit, but honestly, I was quite literally getting stomped until Trenton showed up," he said.

Trenton, getting a kick out of the charming exchange he was witnessing, sported a thumbs up. Being a good sport, he didn't want Bradford to lose the momentum he had with his lady.

"That coffee to the pants was a nice touch, though. Gotta give you credit," he said.

"That was very satisfying to witness," Heather added. She turned to look at their new companions. "What was up with those guys? They were making weird claims about someone getting killed."

"I think it was the Freddy guy's brother," Bradford said. "They seem to think it was us because of yesterday's little spat."

Trenton's face shifted with a hint of amusement and affront. "You suggesting *we* had something to do with that?"

"How can you blame them," Matt commented. "I mean, you go in there all Jason Statham-like, beating up those guys without getting a scratch. Then you pull your secret pistol on them in the end… By the way, you could've led with that. Saved a little time."

"Needed to throw them for a loop first. Plus, I needed the exercise." He looked to the married couple seated in front of him. "To answer your question: no. I'm as unfamiliar with what they were talking about as you."

Bradford nodded. There was still something off with their story, but he decided it was not worth digging into.

All he cared about was getting out of here.

"I see the lake," Heather said.

Bradford brought the vehicle out of the woods near the shoreline, parking next to the orange Dodge Journey.

He honked the horn and watched the lake.

"Where the hell are they?"

Heather's newfound enthusiasm quickly dissipated. "I don't see them."

"Obviously, they're here, because that's their car," Bradford said.

"Maybe they went hiking?" Matt suggested.

Bradford shook his head. "They wouldn't come all the way over to the lake just to go hiking. They would've just gone straight from the camp."

He stepped outside in hopes of getting a better look.

The water was calm, with tiny ripples sweeping onto the shore. In a view like this, two frolicking people splashing about would be impossible to miss.

Heather joined him. "Betty? Shawn?"

"You know them better than I do," he said. "Could they have swum down a ways?"

Heather shook her head. "Not without their raft and their…" She turned her head to look at the inflated raft left behind amongst other gear and refreshments, catching a glimpse of something laying on the shore thirty feet down.

"Brad?"

He turned to look, taking a moment before he saw the thing. Right away, he saw the redness in the water and the sand which had his wife on edge.

Trenton and Matt stepped out, the latter gulping.

"We should go."

Heather and Bradford broke into a sprint to inspect the oddity, stopping after coming within fifteen feet.

Betty's upper half was lying face-up, arms out to the side, her body deflated and pale from loss of blood and organ tissue.

"Oh, God!" Heather dug her face into her husband's chest. He wrapped his arms around her and started backing away, his own panic gradually rising. As they headed back to their vehicle, his eyes went to a small disturbance in the shallows, where the gentle current broke against the mangled corpse of Shawn. His head, shoulders, and the entire left side of his body was intact.

His right leg, hip, and the right side of his torso under his armpit had been ripped away.

Not feeling the need to direct Heather's attention to the horrid sight, he steered her back to the truck.

"You've got your wish," he said to Matt. "We're getting out of here."

"What's going on?" Heather cried. "What did this? Do you two know what's going on?"

They noticed the way Matt looked at Trenton for advice. It was an act that eliminated all doubt that they had knowledge they were not disclosing.

"You guys seriously need to spit it out," Bradford said. His gratefulness for their intervention with the biker gang had run dry. "What's going on? What do you know?"

A series of roaring engines drew all four pairs of eyes to the interior of the woods. Motorcycles were approaching at rapid speed. Several of them. At least ten…

"Shit." Trenton opened the truck door and reached for one of his duffle bags. "I guess they're back for more."

"Get in the truck," Bradford said.

"And go where?" Trenton said. "It's not like you can cut through the forest. The way we need to go is through there." He pointed at the trail; precisely where the rumbling sounds were coming from.

"What if they're armed this time?" Matt said.

"That's what I'm preparing for." He punctuated his statement by revealing his M16 assault rifle.

Bradford and Heather stumbled away from him, stricken by an all new wave of shock.

"What the hell are you doing all the way out here with *that?*" Heather said. If the rifle itself was not intimidating enough, the underbarrel grenade launcher was certainly able to compensate.

Trenton did not bother answering and took a firing position near the truck's engine. Matt backed up near the others, gripping his special briefcase tightly.

A *crash* shook the forest.

Next came a scream.

Then a *smash*, which abruptly ended that screaming, and resulted in other frantic yelling.

Behind the grumbling engines were heavy stomps, getting louder and louder as they neared the lakeside.

"What is that?" Heather gasped.

Trenton rose from his kneeling position, suddenly anxious.

VROOM!

The biker gang tore out of the woods at top speed, many of them looking over their shoulder.

One of them saw the truck directly in front of them and veered sharply, flipping himself over and tumbling into the lake.

There were only five of them, their leader Freddy being the last to emerge. He made eye contact with the group he had clashed with minutes ago, not displaying aggression, but unimaginable fright.

"It's coming!"

Trenton shifted to the lakeshore, cursing between clenched teeth.

"What's coming?" Bradford said.

The answer tore from the tree line, holding two bikers in its large hands. Bradford and Heather shrieked at once, their minds enduring a storm of confusion and terror as they recognized the mythical simian beast standing before them. It was a series of thoughts everyone else who laid eyes on the creature experienced. No matter where one existed on the globe, they had heard the legends. Most believed it to be untrue; nothing more than the figments of vivid imaginations.

But it was real. And it was violent.

It was Bigfoot.

Roaring in fury, the beast bashed the two bikers together, shattering their skeletal structures on impact.

It threw one of their limp corpses at a pair of motorcycles escaping to the right. The one in the front hit the body and flipped over, while the man right behind him attempted to veer out of the way, inadvertently putting himself in the water.

Freddy and the fifth biker attempted to turn left. Their wheels spun uselessly in the sand, failing to get the proper traction.

"Shit…" Freddy looked at the beast. "SHIT!"

Bigfoot came after him, discarding the other dead biker in favor of grabbing him with both hands. Freddy abandoned his bike and ran for the truck, leaving his buddy still trying to drive away on his bike.

The biker yelled, seeing Bigfoot's massive hands nearing his face.

It grabbed him by the shoulder, wrapping its other hand around his face. Twisting like a bottlecap, it snapped the guy's head right off. Pushing his body to the ground, Bigfoot lifted the motorcycle and pivoted towards Freddy.

He looked over his shoulder just in time to see the beast raising the bike.

Bradford, too, recognized the arm motion.

"Look out!"

The group scattered.

Bigfoot launched the motorcycle, crashing it against the hood of the truck with enough force to generate sparks and ignite the bike's ruptured fuel tank.

BOOM!

Vibrations, smoke, and adrenaline led to all sorts of chaos which caused Bradford and Heather to lose their bearings for a few moments. They were running. Which way? They didn't know. Everything was a blur.

They stopped, finding themselves at the tree line.

Gathering their focus, they turned around to gauge the evolving situation.

Bigfoot moved past the flaming truck, chasing the two bikers who had been thwarted by the projectile body of their dead friend.

It picked up the one who had fallen in the sand, watching the way he kicked and screamed within its grasp.

An animalistic smile gave the guy one final jolt of fear before those jaws parted. The man wailed, those jaws closing over his face.

CHOMP!

Bigfoot dropped the dead man, watching the brains spill from his open head.

Next, it went for the biker who fell in the water. The guy attempted to backstroke, his heavy boots and thick jeans weighing him down.

Bigfoot waded in and snatched him up as easily as plucking a koi from a pond. This time, while holding him in front of its face, it decided to end the man's life with a closed fist.

It struck with crushing force, rendering the biker's face and chest to jelly.

The sound of an engine made the beast turn to its left. Freddy, who had managed to avoid the thing after the explosion, had put himself in the driver's seat of Shawn's vehicle, gladly abandoning the last of his companions who still floundered in the lake.

Once again, the beast made use of one of the motorcycles, chucking it at the Dodge with explosive force.

Freddy fell out through the open door, the vehicle imploding behind him.

Lost in a fit of horror, he did the only thing he could think to do. He grabbed one of Betty's inflatable rafts and launched himself into the lake. Lying on his stomach, he paddled with both hands, hoping to get to the opposite shore.

His buddy, unwilling to return to the same beach presently occupied by Bigfoot, reached for the raft.

"Let me on!"

Freddy kicked him in the face. "Get off!"

He resumed stroking, looking back after hearing the splashes of those gargantuan feet coming into the water.

The beast was in the zone, eager to eliminate the remainder of the biker gang as if they were on a checkbox, not willing to tear into the other humans until that box was marked off.

"Fuck!"

Freddy pulled his leg up and gave his follower another kick. It was not because the guy was reaching for his raft—he wasn't—but to leave him dazed long enough to be useful as bait.

It worked.

The man, bleeding from his nose and mouth, screamed as the shadow of the hairy beast encompassed him. Bigfoot lifted him out of the water, twisted his body, then tossed him over his shoulder like trash.

He came down on the shoreline, face-up, getting a view of his boot heels, ass, and corkscrewed middle before slipping eternally into darkness.

Freddy resumed paddling, watching the monster. It waded further into the water, slowing down as it got waist high. With the benefit of the inflatable, he was gradually gaining distance.

"That's right, you furry son of a bitch!" he shouted. "Having a hard time swimming? All that hair weighing you down?" He flipped the bird at Bigfoot, then turned his eyes forward.

He leaned upward, the confidence eliminated by the swirling ripples taking place in front of him.

In the middle of the little whirlpool, a large serpentine shape emerged. It had large round eyes, dark, leathery skin, two fins on each side, huge open jaws revealing razor-sharp fangs, and a gnarly disposition for shredding anything that came within reach.

Freddy yelled.

The inflatable popped, the bottom jaw's fangs ramming through it into his belly. At the same time, the upper jaws hammered his back, staking the long, thin teeth into his flesh.

Bradford and Heather remained at the tree line, gasping at the incredible sight. They were looking at something resembling a sea serpent.

Or an eel.

Its head was fairly round, its texture and eyes fish-like. After seeing the tip of its tail slapping the water, they estimated the thing to be thirty feet long. Snake-like in its basic form, it was flexible, designed for constricting enemies. It was a tactic not needed for Freddy, for it was able to ravage his body with a few squishy chomping motions.

Bigfoot threw its arms out and bellowed.

The eel spat out Freddy's pulped remains and looked at the bipedal challenger. It made no sound, for it lacked vocal cords. Still, its murderous intent was present in its eyes and blood-dripping jaw. Cocking its head back, it resembled a cobra, ready to strike.

Bigfoot waded deeper, pissed that the aquatic foe had stolen its kill. Responding to the presence of the simian, the eel moved into shallower water, its body rippling in swimming motions.

The fight was on.

Bigfoot stopped and braced for the collision, putting its hands forward as the eel lifted its head out of the water to make a bite to the throat. Huge hands seized the aquatic fiend by the neck and wrestled it to the side.

Large jaws snapped shut inches from Bigfoot's face, the long upper body failing to push through the defenses.

Bigfoot drew one of those hands back, clenched a fist, and struck the eel on the snout. It whipped backwards, its body rippling with intense motion. A flick of its tail allowed the eel some distance, avoiding Bigfoot's attempt to grab hold of it again.

It circled back and made a second run at the humanoid. Bigfoot braced again, anticipating a similar attack.

The eel stayed low this time, going for the legs instead of the throat. Bigfoot roared, feeling the teeth puncturing its shin and calf. The eel looped its body around its enemy's knees and waist, tightening in the same manner as a boa constrictor.

Loss of balance caused Bigfoot to throw its arms out in a flimsy manner. A stronger bite from those jaws resulted in an ear-piercing screech and a shift of motion. Unable to make a step, Bigfoot fell to its left, disappearing under a mountain range of rolling waves.

"Hey!"

Bradford and Heather jumped at the sound of Trenton's voice. He approached from their left, with Matt trailing behind him. At some point during the chaos, they had managed to find a place to lay low while Bigfoot handled the bikers.

"Oh, you're alive," Bradford said.

"At the moment," a flustered Matt said. "We lost our ride."

"Doesn't change a thing," Trenton said. "We need to move. Hopefully the fish will take care of the problem for us, but all the same, I don't want to stay here and find out."

"Any ideas where we can go?" Matt said. "How well do you two know this forest?"

Bradford looked past him at the conflict within the lake. Bigfoot was back on its feet, the eel still wrapping itself around its waist. This time, it was biting its shoulder, spilling rivers of blood down the matted coat of fur.

"That place!" Heather said, waving her finger while her brain formed the right sentence structure. "There's a company-owned property at the north end of the lake. Maybe they can help."

"That's got my vote," Bradford said.

"What company?" Matt asked.

Bradford shook his head. "Not sure, to be honest."

"Who cares?" Trenton said. He was watching the battle of titans unfold. "Let's go for it."

Together, they ran north, the married couple suppressing their questions about what Trenton was doing all the way out here with an assault rifle.

Bigfoot bellowed, feeling those teeth digging deeper into its flesh. The eel was without fear or empathy. It attacked with no other objective but to kill.

What it lacked was intelligence; something Bigfoot had in spades. It knew it could not win by wrestling the eel on its own turf. Nor could it inflict a killing blow with brute force like it could do with the humans. Not in this environment, anyway. The eel had a different physicality than land animals. It was able to absorb impact even as vicious as

Bigfoot's punches without sustaining too much damage.

Bigfoot grabbed the thing by its head. Right away, it knew the skull was too thick for it to crush inward.

The jaw, however, was a different story.

It wrestled its mighty hands between the gaps in the eel's teeth and pulled outward, gradually prying them from its flesh. The eel's body tightened around Bigfoot's midsection, driving some of the air from its lungs. It kept up the effort, freeing itself from those little daggers.

The eel tried to force its head forward to secure another bite, but its enemy was unrelenting in its grip. Bigfoot backed up into shallower waters, then used its own body weight to wrestle the eel's head into the soft soil.

Those big eyes twitched in their sockets, the neck twisting and turning in a failed effort to free itself.

Bigfoot pulled farther, revealing the back of the eel's throat to the world. Now, the aquatic predator was shaking out of intense pain.

Relishing in that fact, Bigfoot gave one final yank.

CRACK!

The jaw split, peeling the flesh at the corners of its mouth.

Bigfoot released the lower jaw and plowed his hand into the back of its enemy's throat, seizing the spinal column. With a shaking motion, he separated the skull from the rest of the body.

The eel spasmed, then went still.

Triumphant, Bigfoot uncoiled the thirty-foot corpse from its torso and pushed it onto the beach. It leaned forward and roared in its dead opponent's face, berating it.

The next several minutes were spent catching its breath. Though delighted in its victory, the urge to kill remained.

Bigfoot inspected its surroundings, seeing the dead bikers, wrecked vehicles, and a notable absence of the other four humans in the area.

It exhaled through its nostrils.

They could run, but there was nowhere to hide.

CHAPTER 13

"You hear that?"

Bradford froze, fearing his wife was addressing movement somewhere in the forest. On the contrary, she was looking at the sky.

That did not put him at ease either. For all he knew, in addition to Bigfoot and the monster eel, there could be a giant bird swooping through the trees. Or worse, mosquitos!

In his mind, anything was possible at this point.

What did bring him relief was the familiarity of the sound when he heard it. It was a whirring sound, easily recognizable by even the most common of folk. Whether it was on television or passing overhead in real life, everybody had seen and heard a helicopter at some point in their lives.

This one was flying low, too.

"Maybe it's a company chopper," he said.

"Good!" Heather replied. "Then maybe we can bum a flight out of here!"

The four of them accelerated into a run, weaving between the trees while keeping the lake within view. They did not want to travel along the shoreline out of fear it would make them too easy to spot in case Bigfoot followed. At the same time, it was their primary guide to finding their destination.

"I see a fence," Trenton said, pointing up ahead.

Less than a hundred feet dead ahead was a clearing.

"Oh, yes. Yes!" Matt exclaimed.

They sliced through the section of forest and emerged in the sunshine, the Wynns quick to run to the gate.

"Hello?" Bradford shouted.

"Can anyone help us?" Heather joined in.

Trenton, meanwhile, watched the chopper. He was able to get a glimpse of it as it continued north. It flew at low altitude, yet did not appear to have any relation to this facility.

"Huh?" Matt said. "They're flying awfully low. Maybe there's a landing pad somewhere else."

Trenton looked at the complexity of the facility on the other side of the fence. "Why would they put the money in all of this, yet not bother installing a landing pad for their chopper here, where it's convenient?"

The next question came after noticing the state of the place and a rotten odor permeating the air.

Bradford and Heather stepped away from the fence, unnerved by the sight of a huge gap in the main building. It was two stories high and leaning heavily in their direction, a huge part of its base blown out onto the grass from an explosive impact inside.

Further inspection of the property led to the discovery of the dome-shaped structure on the west side, and the small trail leading from the breach in its roof, under the fence, into the lake. It was a trail that reminded them of a line of slime left by a slug, only much larger.

"That's where the eel came from," Heather concluded. "This is where they *both* came from."

Bradford took a breath. "What the hell were they doing out here?"

"Maybe we're better off not going in," Heather suggested.

Trenton went up to the gate and took a look for himself. "Either we find something gnarly in here, or we continue to wander in Monster Forest. I'll take my chances with this place."

He went around the west corner and made his way to the small gap dug out under the fence where the eel had escaped.

"You coming?" he said after pausing to look at Matt.

Matt did not appear to be too keen on going in there, but he also wanted the protection of Trenton's firearms. Clinging to the sense of security, he trotted after his partner.

For a short while, the Wynns remained at the south fence, unsure if they wanted to venture into the complex.

Bradford looked at Heather, seeing she still had Betty's pistol tucked in her jean shorts.

"Don't lose that," he said.

"How dumb do you think I am?" she replied.

Bradford smiled at her. "I don't think you're dumb at all. I just really want you to stay safe, is all."

Heather's expression softened at the sound of those words. She touched his arm, giving him an electrified feeling he had not felt in a while.

"Maybe this is a bad time for me to bring this up… you know, with us getting chased by monsters and everything… but I've been worried you haven't been happy in our marriage lately."

Bradford chuckled. "Yes, it is a bad time to bring it up." She snickered at that. "But, no. I've been kinda missing the way things used to be, but I don't regret marrying you one bit. I've been feeling a little insecure lately." He tapped his stomach and his thinning hair. "I'm not exactly trophy husband material. I feel like I'm aging like milk, and you've been put off by it."

"What?" She touched his face. "Is that what's been bothering you?"

"Let's face it. I was in great shape when we dated and got married. Now look at me. I'm the guy who ate your husband."

Heather gave him a light, playful smack. "Don't be ridiculous!" She poked his stomach. "You're acting like you're morbidly obese. You've put on maybe twenty pounds. Twenty-five at most. I still think you're as handsome as ever. You're my man. All this time, I've been worried you've been put off by me."

"Huh?" Bradford put a hand on her chin. "Are you for real?"

"Yes. I mean, I'm not exactly as slim as I used to be. I'm starting to get some wrinkles going, some lines that I wish would go away…"

"Hey, you're the woman who gave me three beautiful, maybe troublesome, but still beautiful boys," he said. "I guess, we haven't taken well to this whole 'getting older' thing."

"I guess nobody really does," she said. "What about me not becoming a lawyer?"

"You're asking me if I'm bothered?" Bradford asked. "No, of course not. I mean, if you wanna try and make another go for it, I'm here for you."

"Really?" She beamed a smile at him. Bradford had done the impossible—he had made her forget about a killer rampaging Bigfoot, even if only for a moment. "I was think of doing just that, but I thought you wouldn't like it."

He shook his head. "You can count on me. Here I was, thinking you thought little of me and my job all this time."

"Why would I think that?" she said. "You pay the bills, have a retirement account, aren't burying us in unnecessary credit card debt. I don't care what you do for a living… as long as it's not stripping."

Bradford snorted. "Oh, darn. So much for my dream."

Laughing, the two of them embraced with a hug and a kiss.

"Eh-hem!"

They looked through the fence, seeing Matt staring back at them. If there was anything more shocking to him than man-eating beasts, it was seeing them rekindling their love an hour after watching a whole bike gang get massacred.

"You guys gonna stay out there, or…?"

Heather nodded. "Yeah, let's head through the gate."

Holding hands, they made their way to the opening where the eel had slipped through. The tunnel was large enough to enable them to get to the other side by ducking as opposed to army crawling.

Now inside the campus, they got a closer view of the aftermath of what had occurred. They saw the trailers, the radio shack, dome, and garage. A couple of company jeeps had been crushed, they assumed by Bigfoot's fists, going by the size and shape of the indents. The radio shack had been pummeled pretty good as well.

To the north was something that really alarmed them. Heather gasped and reached for her pistol, refraining from pulling it out after seeing that the thing was dead.

Like most people, she hated rats to begin with. Giant rats were even worse. The one lying a few dozen meters from a breach in the north fence was dead, as was a second one lying near one of the buildings. Their heads had been smashed in by a blunt force.

Bradford cringed, envisioning Bigfoot laying waste to the creature by hammering its skull with its fist.

Trenton stepped away from the dome's main entrance, holding his rifle in the same manner as an active-duty Marine securing an area.

"There's a huge pool in there," he said, pointing his elbow at the structure. "That's where they kept the fish friend until things went sour."

"Good to know," Matt said. "But that doesn't answer the question: why the hell would someone be housing Bigfoot, a giant eel, and a bunch of super rats out here in the middle of nowhere? And what the hell else did they have here?"

Heather shuddered, tightly gripping her husband's arm as she looked to the southeast. "I think I know…"

She pointed a shaky finger.

All eyes turned in that direction. Shockingly, they had all missed it when they came in. Now, they could not *unsee* it.

It was a transparent net, most visible when direct light was set on it. It stretched from one of the trailers to the main building, quivering slightly as a breeze passed through it.

Matt's face turned a shade of green. "Is that what I think it is?"

Bradford focused on the funnel-shaped things held in the middle of the net. They were weaved from the same thready material, though with many more layers. Behind the white sheets were pale human faces.

Heather turned away. "Oh, my…" She hunched over, on the verge of vomiting. She took a few deep breaths and regained control. It helped that she had skipped breakfast that morning.

"Oh, Jesus," Bradford exclaimed. He could see movement coming from the corners of the nest. The grey bodies moving overtop the cocoons were segmented into two parts; a head and bulky abdomen. Eight legs stretched from their middle, carrying them from one point of the nest to another.

One was hunched near one of the cocoons, pulsing slightly, the victim giving off a haunting moan.

Matt began to sway. Bradford caught him before he could fall.

"They're still alive," Matt groaned. "The spiders are… eating them."

Trenton watched, his mind still registering what he was looking at. "Talk about a shitty way to go out."

"We've got to help them," Bradford said.

Trenton scoffed. "Yeah, sure. Be my guest."

Bradford moved over to his wife. "Give me the gun."

Still fighting to keep from passing out, she passed it over to him. "We should leave."

"Not without doing what we can," he said. "Besides, I don't want to walk through the woods knowing *these things* exist."

He ran towards the nest, waving at Trenton.

"Great," the guy moaned. "Well, if you're going to piss those things off…"

He ran after Bradford.

Both men stopped eighteen feet away from the web. The sight of dried, cocoon husks lying on the ground gave them pause, especially after seeing the skeletal corpses trapped inside.

There were five spiders moving to the center of the nest, all watching the new arrivals with their eight eyes. They were eight feet in body length, their leg span twice that.

"I hate spiders!" Trenton exclaimed. He pointed his rifle and hit one of them with a three-round burst, exploding its head into a tidal wave of green mush.

He shifted the muzzle to the left and hit the next one. Its exoskeleton burst easily, erasing all of its facial features and spilling the insides of its head onto the grass and concrete.

Bradford aimed the late Betty's pistol at the one farthest to the left. He fired a shot. There was no reaction by the spider; no sign of any damage. Inside, he was cursing at himself. *How can you miss that huge thing?*

He took another shot. A jet of green blood popped from its abdomen. The spider leaned its front half upward, its legs slashing at the air.

Stricken by terror, Bradford fired again, planting the bullet through its belly. Three more shots struck its face, putting an end to its protest.

He lowered the gun, the tension proving more exhausting than all of the running he had done up until now.

Trenton planted several rounds through the remaining two arachnids. Their body parts rolled down the height of the nest, many of them sticking to the strands.

He lowered the rifle and loaded a fresh magazine.

"Happy now?"

Bradford's eyes combed over the web, confirming no more of those ugly things were hiding somewhere. He focused on one of the cocoons. The man inside was shifting. They were weak motions, but enough to confirm there was still life in the guy.

He approached the nest, recoiling after attempting to touch it.

"Ya might wanna remember the rule of spiderwebs, Bradford," Trenton said.

"Right." Bradford kept his hands away. "They're meant for capturing prey." He turned to his right, spotting the garage.

He ran through its open door and searched inside. Unlike the high-tech look of the other buildings, it was a typical maintenance building, complete with all sorts of tools, air conditioning equipment, and a forklift!

Bradford got into the vehicle, started it up, and drove it outside into the open. He raised the fork to its twelve-foot maximum height, then drove straight to the spiderweb.

Muttering "Ah, hell," Trenton got out of the way.

Bradford impaled the web with the fork, making sure to avoid the prisoners strapped to it. He shifted the lever, lowering the fork to the ground. The web stretched downward, lowering the five prisoners until the webs covering their feet were touching the grass.

Having summoned her courage, Heather joined her husband at the web. He passed her some utility gloves and some tools he had taken from the garage, then got to work cutting through some of the cocoons.

The first person they freed was dead, his blood having been drained.

Bradford, gulping hard, moved to the next one. Sadly, she was in the same condition.

Heather worked on the two on the left, shaking her head at Bradford. They, too, had passed on.

They met in the middle, using pliers and wire cutters to reveal the face of the fifth and final hostage.

Inside was a man in his late forties. His face was a shade of white, though not quite as pasty as his deceased colleagues. His hair was starting to fall out and his face looked as weak as tissue paper.

Bradford touched the man's face. "Hello? Sir? Wake up! Are you alright?"

The man twitched.

Bradford tried again. "Come on. Wake up."

Heather started cutting away at more of the cocoon. At his torso, the webbing was thicker and much tougher to cut.

"I can't get it," she said.

"First thing's first," Trenton said. "Try and get him to talk."

Agreeing with that sentiment, Bradford tapped the man's face again. "Sir, wake up. We're here to help."

The man turned his head, twitched his lips, and after a minute, opened his eyes. He looked at the people in front of him, gasping in surprise.

"Shh! Shh!" Heather said. "It's okay."

The man looked left and right, mouth in a crooked position. "W-where is she?"

"Who?" Heather asked.

"They're all dead," Trenton said. "All of your staff, they're dead." He noticed the looks he got from Heather and Bradford. "He was gonna have to find out sometime."

"Ooohhh… but…" Every word came out as a moan. "The arachnids…"

"They're dead," Bradford said, reassuringly. "We killed them all."

"All?"

Trenton sported his M16 as though it was a hunting rifle. "It got a little sporty."

"Ooohhh."

Bradford was unsure if the man was in pain or not. "We'll get you out of here. I promise. We just need to find the right tools to cut you free."

"What the hell is this place?" Trenton said. "Beg your pardon, but this doesn't strike me as a typical nature reserve. So far, we've seen giant rats, giant eels, giant spiders, and fucking Bigfoot. Going by the looks of this place, it all originated here."

The man stared blankly, his mind slowly reactivating. "It was a project. We thought we were doing something great. But now, we're paying the price." He looked Bradford in the eye. "It's a curse. A curse!"

Bradford's mouth jittered as if he was standing in freezing cold temperatures.

"A curse?"

"Bigfoot's curse!" the man said, possibly delirious.

"Before you spill the beans, I just want to know one thing," Trenton said. "Are there any more oversized critters we should be worried about?"

The man shook his head. "No. Spiders, the eel, rats… and *him*."

Trenton snorted. "Him. Bigfoot, of course." He looked at the main building. "So, this place is a big lab, am I right?"

The man nodded. "We were developing new strains of—"

"Got it." He looked at the Wynns. "You guys can continue this chat. I need to take care of something." He turned around and walked over to Matt. "I need to borrow that briefcase."

"What for?"

"I just want to check something."

Bradford and Heather shared a glance, each unsure what was bothering their new so-called friend.

"I didn't mean for this to happen," the man said.

"It's okay," Heather assured him. "We'll get you out of here."

"No… I deserve it." The man groaned, visibly in discomfort. "My name is Dr. Elrond Sachel. I am a geneticist who was hired by Rain to study the effects of the blood."

Heather and Bradford watched in stunned silence. Simultaneously, they asked, "Blood?"

"The blood of Bigfoot," Dr. Sachel replied.

Bradford looked at the corpses of the arachnids, then over at the dead rats.

"Wait…. Bigfoot's *blood* is what caused this?"

Sachel nodded, eyes closed. "Five years ago, it appeared in a different forest. It awoke with a rampage, killing everything in sight. We believe it underwent a hibernation, hence it had not been seen for at least half a century prior to that point."

Heather felt her throat go dry. "My lord…"

"So, it's real?"

"It's real," Dr. Sachel said. "Unfortunately for many people, it's real. The monster killed without mercy. It slaughtered anything it came across, human, animal, it did not matter. It is an intelligent beast too, knowing how to hunt, hide, strategize, even cook!"

"But why is it here?" Bradford asked. "What is it about the blood that makes Bigfoot so special that a company would make all of this?" He waved his hand at all of the buildings and equipment around them.

"That is Bigfoot's curse," Sachel groaned. "It's the blood—the blood of Bigfoot has mutagenic properties. If its blood connects with the circulatory system of another living thing, it alters the DNA. The subject, depending on the amount of exposure, may change in a matter of minutes or hours. In most cases, the change happens within forty minutes."

"Hold on," Heather said. "You're saying Bigfoot had mutant blood?"

"That's his curse," the scientist said. He inhaled deeply through his nostrils. "Five years ago, a band of police officers were searching for some missing persons. A massacre took place. One of the people in the group was exposed to the blood. It had entered through an open wound of his. After a while, the man reportedly changed. When his body was found, he was in an altered condition, having grown in size and strength... and rage. He became more powerful than any human on earth, but in his hubris, he tried to take on the beast itself. Against the father of his enhancement, the mutant man was no match. It killed him and resumed its rampage."

"What happened after that?" Bradford asked. "Obviously, the monster was stopped and brought here."

Sachel nodded.

"There was a fire. They thought Bigfoot was dead, but it escaped. After the debriefing from the survivors, my company sent some operatives in. Twelve of them were killed in the hunt. Bigfoot proved resilient to the sedatives, requiring a heavy dose relative to his mass to bring it down. But we got him out of there. The massacre was given a few different cover stories. Some said it was a raging grizzly bear on the loose. Others said it was a serial killer. The survivors, knowing they would be locked away in a mental institution, decided to keep the truth hidden. They accepted a payment from the company and were relocated to an undisclosed location, equally quiet to the place they lived before."

"But why?" Heather asked. "I mean, why study the monster's blood?"

"To know more about it," Sachel said in a tone extremely lucid compared to the weak drawl he spoke in up to this point. "The beast is believed to be hundreds of years old. Maybe thousands. It can sleep for decades at a time. If we could harvest its abilities, we could improve the human condition. Solve the stasis issue for space travel. Cure diseases. Increase lifespans."

Now, it was Bradford who was feeling sick. The way the doctor spoke, he was not just explaining what he was working on out here; he was trying to convince them he was *right* to do it. Even now, while he was wrapped in a cocoon produced by one of his test subjects, he believed in his work and felt the need to justify it to these two strangers standing in front of him.

"For a long time, we managed to keep the monster hidden. We drew his blood, ran tests, watched so many different species change as a result. Almost all of them needed to be put down. No matter how we tried to alter the compound carried in its bloodstream, the subjects grew and became more violent."

"And they broke out," Bradford concluded.

"Bigfoot broke out," Sachel said. "The damage it caused started a chain reaction. Every specimen in the complex entered an uncontrollable rage. All of them got loose and attacked the staff. The eel, the rats, the spiders… Mother…"

Bradford raised an eyebrow. "Sorry?"

"Your mother was here?" Heather asked.

"No…" Sachel swayed his head back and forth, his mind retreating into deliriousness again. "Not mother… *Mother!*"

Bradford looked at his wife, not liking what he was hearing. There was no point in asking, as the guy's mind was slipping away again. But there was something he was trying to convey. Something important.

Bradford found himself gripping his pistol tighter. With caution, he moved around the long web net, giving himself a view of the one part of the property he had not properly viewed.

On the east side, between the perimeter fence and the main compound, a large funnel-shaped web protruded from the ground. Sticking out of its wide entrance were several grey legs. It was at least five times the size of the 'little ones' he and Trenton had shot down.

Bradford had never pissed himself in his life, but this moment was the closest he came.

Out of breath, he nearly backed into the web.

"What is it?" Heather asked. "What do you see?"

Barely keeping up with the rushing of blood through his veins, Bradford made his way to where she stood.

"We need to get this guy off this web *now*."

"What's the matter?" Heather moved to the right to get a look at whatever had her husband unnerved. After laying eyes on the funnel, she understood. "Oh!"

"Get him off! Get him off!" Bradford whispered, trying to use the wire cutters to slice through the web. "We're damn lucky the thing didn't wake up to all the shooting."

"How are we going to get out of here?" Heather asked.

"You saw that propane truck?" Bradford said.

"Yeah. I also saw that it has a flat tire."

"Yeah? You rather just chance it on foot?" Bradford said.

Heather paused, feeling foolish from voicing her concern. "Nope! Not at all." From behind them came shuffling footsteps from a very nervous Matt Bing. "Guys?"

They could barely make out what he was saying through his very low whisper.

"What?" Heather said.

Matt squirmed and put a finger to his lips. "Shh!" He pointed his thumb to the south gate, mouthing *"It's there!"*

Bradford moved away from the cocoon, stepping just around the corner of one of the trailers to get a peek.

There Bigfoot was, thumping its feet, moving along the fence line.

Bradford pulled away, gritting his teeth. "Shit!"

Now it was clear who won the spat between it and the eel. Bradford was rooting for the latter. At least that thing would've remained in the lake instead of chasing them through the woods.

He tiptoed over to the forklift, where Heather and Matt were huddled. "It doesn't know we're here. Let's cut him loose, and—"

"Matt? Where'd you go?" Trenton shouted from the laboratory's west entrance.

A roar from Bigfoot filled the air, alerting the man with the assault rifle of its presence.

"WHOA!"

Bigfoot stomped its feet and grabbed at the fence. With ease, it created a gap in the metal grid.

"Let's go!" Trenton shouted.

"Not yet!" Heather replied. "We still need to get the doctor loose..."

A hissing sound from the east fence line made her lock up. Matt, unaware of the mother's existence, went over to take a look for himself. "Holy freaking moly!"

As if eight-foot spiders weren't bad enough.

He retreated to the small road running through the middle of the compound. "I'm never going camping ever again! Give me cities, give me criminals, murders, rapists... all of it! At least I won' t have to deal with a giant spider!"

"Giant spider? We killed them all," Trenton said.

Matt frantically pointed.

From around the main lab building, the enormous arachnid's front legs appeared. They bent at their joints, carrying her massive body around the corner. She turned to her right, laying all eight of her eyes on the flabbergasted humans on the other side of the web her younglings had intricately weaved.

Trenton was caught between the shock of seeing her and that of Bigfoot tearing through the fence.

Thinking quickly, he yelled out, "Get your asses in that propane truck!"

He shoved the briefcase in Matt's hands. Even with two beasts nearing him, the guy tried to open it to get a peek at its contents.

Trenton glared at him. "You not trust me?"

"I—of course I do!" Realizing the stupidity of what he was doing, Matt resecured the case.

"Go! Get in the truck!" Trenton said to him. He looked at Heather and Bradford. "You too!"

Bradford was still trying to cut through the thick web. It became obvious why they had tested Bigfoot's blood on spiders: their web, in thick strands, was stronger than steel!

The spider turned the corner, her mandibles rubbing against one another, dripping thick strands of saliva. They parted, revealing two six-foot black fangs.

Now Bradford had given up.

"I'm sorry!"

He and his wife backpedaled from the next, unable to take their eyes off the horrible fate of Dr. Elrond Sachel.

He was squirming in his cocoon, sensing the spider closing in on him. His mouth parted and a husky scream tore into the souls of everyone nearby.

The spider moved over him and extended her fangs horizontally. At once, they slashed downward, cutting through the web and impaling the doctor.

A grotesque slurping sound generated from the cocoon, with the doctor making a gurgling noise while his body literally shrank.

The spider leaned down, taking in the fluids from her creator's body. Once finished, she released her fangs and used her forelegs to pull down the troublesome web separating her from the four humans in her path.

Bradford took Heather's hand and raced to the propane truck.

"Oh, shit!" Matt yelled to them. "Are the keys still in it?"

Bradford hurried to the cab of the truck, hoping the answer was *Yes*.

It wasn't.

"Shit!"

He slammed a fist on the dashboard. Heather, standing right behind him, looked to a pair of bodies lying in the grass on the west side of the road. They both wore grey uniforms with the same company logo that was on the truck.

"One of them has to have the keys!"

Bradford hopped off the truck and started to run for the bodies, only to dig his heels into the ground when he saw the enormous spider scurrying towards him.

She moved slowly, not savoring the experience, but exercising caution, well aware of the threat lingering near the compound.

That threat was Bigfoot.

She turned around, sensing the humanoid monstrosity widening the gap in the fence to allow itself in.

Bigfoot marched onto the roadway, each footstep coming down hard enough to crack the thin pavement.

The spider bent all eight of her legs, ready to launch the attack on her foe. Bigfoot stopped, not out of intimidation, but to psyche itself up for its next brawl. Its injuries from the clash with the eel were minor flesh wounds. The amount of time between that conflict and this one was plenty enough for it to reenergize.

It bellowed, unaware that the eight-legged freak standing before it felt no fear. The only thing going through her simple brain were calculations on how to best get her venom into its bloodstream and paralyze it with a neurotoxin. After which, she would cocoon the beast and keep it fresh until she was ready to feed.

With that in mind, she initiated the fight.

Her back legs propelled her forward like a grasshopper, tackling Bigfoot to the pavement. The simian monster grunted from the impact and roared in defiance. Two mighty hands thrust upward, grabbing ahold of her black, drooling fangs, stopping them within an inch of its chest.

Taking advantage of the two creatures' distraction with one another, Bradford and Heather went to check the bodies of the propane drivers. They recoiled at first, unused to touching a cold human corpse with flies buzzing around them.

Overcoming their anxiety, they started sorting through the pockets.

"Whoa!" Bradford jumped away from the one he was checking, avoiding the rolling mass of the big spider. Bigfoot had kicked her off, sending her rolling like a bowling ball.

She flipped herself right side up and scurried over to Bigfoot for another assault.

The humanoid was prepared this time. It moved to its right, taking itself towards the nest where her younglings had perished. The arachnid adjusted course, fangs horizontal, ready to be rammed into her enemy's furry abdomen.

It played right into Bigfoot's plan.

Grabbing ahold of the forklift, the centuries old beast made a swing at the spider, cracking the cab against her face. She leaned to the side, her legs folding underneath her.

Bigfoot raised the forklift high over its head like a kettlebell, using gravity to let it come down on the spider's head.

She rippled from the impact, her left legs lying flat to the side.

Bigfoot raised the forklift again in the same manner, repeating the same attack.

The spider rolled to her left and slashed with two of her legs. Their tips caught Bigfoot across the face, sending it stumbling backward. The weight held above its head solidified its literal downfall. Unable to keep a grip on the forklift, Bigfoot's grip slipped. The vehicle came down on its forehead, putting it on its back.

All eight legs touched the ground, lifting the spider up. A rippling soundwave spewed from her mandibles while they twitched, dripping fluid.

She came at the beast, her forelegs coming down on its groin.

Bigfoot shot upright with an air-shattering shriek. It threw its two arms out, catching those fangs for the second time.

The spider pedaled her legs, forcing herself forward and laying Bigfoot flat on its back. With the beast at her mercy, she jabbed its neck and chest with her feet, marking its flesh.

Bigfoot endured the pain, baring teeth and keeping those fangs away from its flesh. It tried to bring its feet up to kick her off similarly as last time. Her abdomen was lower, preventing its knees from rising out properly.

She put all of her weight down, inching those fangs closer to that meaty throat below their tips. Drops of venom trickled from their tips, wetting its fur.

The beast looked her in those eight ugly eyes. Anger ran through its veins like steroids, increasing its willpower.

Bigfoot pushed up, creating distance between those black daggers and its neck.

Rolling its hips, it shifted the spider to the right, freeing up enough space to bring one of its legs up and prop its heel under her belly.

A kick launched the spider off of Bigfoot. She landed on her back, legs clawing at the air.

Hissing and screeching, she started to right herself. A blow from a rigid object flattened her on her back once more.

With her eyes pressed against the dirt, the spider was unaware of the forklift being raised over her body. This time, the forks were pointed downward.

Bigfoot slammed the machine into her abdomen.

She lurched, the forks cutting through her belly into the dirt behind her.

Huffing and puffing, Bigfoot stepped back, watching the spider thrashing in a failed attempt to unpin herself from the earth. Green blood spewed from her body, the cracks in her exoskeleton spreading the more she writhed.

"Holy dear God," Bradford said, captivated by the horrific clash he was witnessing.

"I got em!" Heather shouted, pulling keys from one of the worker's pockets.

"Great!" Matt said. "Let's go. We're outta—" He looked around, noticing a particular absence. "Trenton?"

"Is he in the truck?" Heather asked.

Bradford went to check. "Not in here."

"Trenton?" Matt shouted. "Where'd you go, dude?"

A grunt from Bigfoot alerted them to the conclusion of the brawl. The beast had gone back to the spider. With hate in its eyes, it twisted the forklift, cracking her abdomen wide open.

The spider's legs locked in a half-coiled position, holding that pose for several moments before folding all the way to her underside.

Bigfoot watched, victorious, as the life left her body.

"Guys, you do realize we're next, right?" Matt said.

Bradford looked around. "Trenton?"

The guy was nowhere to be seen, having literally disappeared.

Heather watched the humanoid beast. "We can't wait, Brad."

Seeing the dead spider, he nodded in agreement. He hated leaving another person behind. It felt inhuman. At the same time, he was not willing to sacrifice his wife because a guy he had known for a couple of hours decided to run off.

"Get in! Now!"

They piled into the vehicle.

Bradford started it up and hooked it around, putting it through the gap in the north fence. He fought against the wheel to keep the vehicle on point, the flat tire causing it to drag to the side.

They exited the complex and were on the main road, on the way to safety.

On the other side of that fence behind them, Bigfoot roared in anger. Exhausted from the fight with the arachnid, it could do nothing but watch as they vanished into the distance.

CHAPTER 14

Heather leaned across the center console, planting her head lovingly on her husband's shoulder. Bradford's head steadied from the insanity they had recently endured, the endorphins generated by the connection with his wife overpowering all of the angst and dread he experienced throughout the day.

"This was a hell of a vacation, wasn't it?" he said to her.

"Not exactly my favorite," she replied.

"Same here." Bradford took a deep breath. "We'll have crazy stories to tell the kids."

Heather tried not to laugh. After all, several people had died as a result of those mutations roaming the forest, one of which was her coworker. Maybe it was a way of emotionally compensating, but she had to laugh at Bradford's joke.

"You're terrible."

"I suppose I am," he replied. The next breath was a sigh. "On a serious note, I'm not looking forward to explaining to the authorities what happened back there."

"Best we can do is tell them to find the company grounds," Heather suggested. "Once they head over there, they'll see it for themselves. Better yet, they won't get ambushed by giant spiders."

"I always say it's good to be a 'glass half-full' kind of guy," he quipped. He watched the road, dreading the rumbling sound underneath the vehicle.

Matt shifted in the backseat, watching the painfully slow rate in which they moved.

"Do you usually drive like a granny?"

"What do you expect?" Heather said. "One of the tires is flat. We push it too hard, we'll be riding on the rim."

"We practically are," he said. "I'm not pushing it unless I see Bigfoot closing in on my rearview mirror like the T-rex in *Jurassic Park*."

Matt sat back, frustrated, but unable to argue against his logic.

"Sorry about your friend," Heather said to him.

Matt put his hands on his briefcase. "Yeah, thanks."

"Were you guys close?"

Matt rolled his jaw, unsure of how to answer that. "Not really. We were more business associates than pals."

"Oh, I see," Heather said. "Still, I feel bad. I hope you don't hold it against us for leaving him behind. Now that I'm thinking about it, it's starting to weigh on me."

"Me too," Bradford said. He checked his mirrors. "I keep hoping I'll see him running up. We're going slow enough for him to keep pace if he ran. The guy's in pretty damn good shape. He beat up all those biker guys, for crying out loud."

"True," Heather said. "Plus, he has that gun." She went silent, thinking about that oddity. She turned to look at Matt. "Why does he have that gun?

A pistol all the way out here is one thing, but a rifle like that?"

"Hell, I'd even be somewhat willing to accept someone having an M16," Bradford said. "Sorta. But that grenade launcher? What's up with that?" He shifted his mirror so he could see Matt. In the reflection, he took notice of that briefcase. "What's in that thing? You've been favoring it like it's your own child."

"None of your business," Matt said. His defensive tone got Bradford and his wife more curious.

"It's not clothes or other regular belongings," she said. "You dropped your other duffle bags back there. But that briefcase? You seem more willing to lose a hand than lose that thing."

"If I had something of such great value that I was sneaking through the woods, I'd carry an assault rifle too," Bradford commented.

"It's nothing too important," Matt said.

Heather sniggered at that. "Hence, your total willingness to tell us what it is."

Matt looked her in the eye. "It. Is. Not. Your. Concern."

"Right." Bradford shook his head and rolled his eyes. He decided to drop the subject. Matt wasn't going to answer, and the ride was going to be slow and tedious enough. The last thing he needed was to be arguing with the guy over details that did not concern him anyway.

Heather suddenly leaned forward. "What was that?"

Bradford exhaled. *Please not another monster.*

She pointed to the right, just within the trees up ahead. "Something moved. I think it was a person."

Bradford eased on the brakes. "Trenton?"

BANG! BANG! BANG! BANG!

Sparks flew off the hood of the truck. Holes popped in the windshield. The other tires went flat, and metal *CLANGS* vibrated throughout the truck.

Bradford put his wife's head down.

"Holy shit! What the hell?"

Matt tucked himself down as well. "Shit! Shit! Shit! I don't wanna die!"

"Why the hell is he shooting at us?" Heather shouted.

Bradford strained, listening to bullets striking the vehicle on both sides at once.

"That's not him. Those are multiple shooters."

As soon as he made that realization, the blasting ceased.

Bradford waited a few moments, then slowly put his head up. They had deliberately aimed high and low when shooting the cab, and also avoided hitting the tank to avoid an explosion.

Whoever was out there, they wanted them alive.

From the left of the road, a man in tactical gear stepped onto the road. He held a fancy looking automatic rifle in his hands, pointed low while he put himself in front of the vehicle.

"Trenton Loar! Step on out!"

Heather wheezed. These guys meant business and did not know their target was not in the truck.

"He's not here," she whispered to Bradford.

"I know!" he hissed.

The man outside tapped his foot. "We've got multiple guns on you, Trenton. Best show yourself now, or we'll start blasting away at the tank. All that firepower hitting it at once, we're bound to get a spark that'll ignite its contents."

Bradford shifted to get an eye on Matt. "Who are these guys?"

Matt had his hands over his head. "I think it's a man named Bennett. If it's not already obvious, he's a merc."

"How the hell did they find you all the way out here?" Heather said. "I mean, we're driving in a propane truck in the middle of nowhere. Do they have a satellite on you or something?"

"How the hell should I know?" Matt exclaimed. "Do I look like I'm in the 'Killers R Us' business?"

Bradford shook his head. *No, but your buddy Trenton does. And something tells me he knew these guys were nearby.*

He rolled down his window and put a hand out, signaling peace. "I'm not him! I'm coming out! Please do not shoot me. Or my wife. We're not associated with your man."

Heather sat up, but not before taking notice of her husband sneaking Betty's pistol under the driver's seat.

"What are you doing?"

"Until we can prove otherwise, these guys think we're hostile," he said. "Having the gun is not going to improve matters. And despite how well I kick our sons and nephews' asses on *Call of Duty*, I'm not actually a crack shot."

With the gun hidden, he opened his door.

Heather opened her side and stepped out, hands raised.

They touched down on the pavement, keeping calm as five other mercenaries emerged from hiding. They assembled near the vehicle, rifles pointed at the two strangers.

"Anyone else?" the man named Bennett asked.

Bradford tilted his head backward at the truck. "Back seat. Some guy named Matt Bing."

"Oh, thanks!" Matt called out.

"Like they weren't gonna find you anyway," Heather shouted.

Two of the mercenaries moved to the passenger door and dragged the guy out. One of them wrestled his briefcase away from him; something Matt determinedly tried to fight against. A blow to the head with a rifle butt cut his resistance short.

Dropped to one knee, Matt watched as Bennett lifted his briefcase.

"You seriously thought you were gonna get away with it, didn't you?" the mercenary leader said. "Helping Trenton kill your boss. That's low. Ennio Vogler kept you employed for years. He paid for your sister's cancer treatment. He treated you well, in spite of what you might think."

"He double-crossed Trenton," Matt said. "Nobody does that and lives. Not even Ennio."

"I'll hand it to Trenton," Bennett continued. "He did a hell of a number on that mansion. No average man, not even a hitman, can take out that many people singlehandedly. Then again, it wasn't singlehandedly, was it?"

Matt shrugged. "*Mostly* singlehandedly. I was just the driver. The others had small roles in making it so we could escape easily. One person had a safehouse. But it doesn't matter now."

"Why not?"

Matt looked up at him. "Because they're dead."

Bennett lifted a finger to Heather and Bradford. "It wasn't these two?"

Matt shook his head. "They don't even know what we're talking about. We ran into them after our ride got battered."

Bennett and his team looked at each other and started laughing.

"You smashed up your getaway ride? My God, Matt, you're a driver. You'd think you'd be more careful, especially if you're trying to flee for your life. What? You take your eyes off the wheel and crash into a tree? That why your pals are dead?"

Matt bobbed his head and scoffed.

"Believe me, trees have been the least of my problems today."

"How did your friends die? In the crash?"

"You'll laugh if I told you," Matt replied.

Bennett was laughing already. "What about Trenton? Where is he?"

Matt shook his head. "Why bother telling you? You'll just shoot me anyway. That's what you've been paid to do. I'm not the brightest bulb, but I'm not brain dead."

Bennett and the other team members shared some chuckles. "Technically, I was paid to kill Trenton Loar and *find out* who he was working with… but yeah, Ennio's brother would probably have you killed too. The question is; will it be slow? Or fast?"

One of the mercenaries grabbed ahold of Heather and placed a gun to her head.

Bradford rushed forward with a speed and strength he didn't know he possessed, smacking the gun away and hitting the man in the nose.

One of the others came up from behind him and cracked a rifle butt against the back of his head, dropping him.

He was lifted right back up and slammed against the truck. Heather was placed next to him, breathing heavily, watching at the gun muzzles pointed at them.

"Sorry you two got mixed up in this," Bennett said. "Not sure what else to say. Other than you should've vacationed somewhere else."

"Personally, I would've preferred the casino myself," Bradford remarked.

Bennett appreciated the humor in that remark. "Same here." He grabbed Matt by the collar of his shirt and pinned him against the front of the truck. "I know you're no angel. You worked for a drug lord, for crying out loud. But you've always been the kind of guy who preferred to stay out of the real messy part of the business. Never had a stomach for it. And that's okay, not everyone is meant to. *But…* you did something stupid by linking arms with Trenton Loar. So now, you're going to tell me where he is. And if you don't…"

He looked at the female member of his team. She put her rifle to Bradford's forehead and started squeezing the trigger. At the last second, she jerked the gun skyward.

BANG!

Bradford jolted, feeling the heat from the muzzle flare.

"That's just the warning shot," Bennett said to Matt. "Next one will be messier. Might not lead right to death—might take three, four, five… who knows? Maybe even six shots to get it right."

Matt was breathing heavily. If there was anything to be known about Bennett, it was that he did not bluff.

He looked at his new companions, watching them stand bravely without giving their potential killers the satisfaction of fear.

A day or so ago, he would have balked about putting himself in harm's way for a stranger. Today, it was a different story. Then again, were these people still strangers? Was knowing someone for a couple of hours, avoiding biker gangs and killer bigfoots enough to graduate from the 'stranger' phase?

Whatever the answer was, one thing was clear: he didn't lack the heart to let them die for his sake. And definitely not Trenton's.

"There's a facility a half mile back that way," he said. "We just got away from there. Had we not had a flat, we'd be miles down the road by now."

"You left him there?" Bennett asked.

"He vanished while we were trying to get on out of there," Matt explained.

"Sounds like you were in quite a hurry," Bennett said. "You get testy with the staff?"

"That's a whole other story," Matt said. "Only way you're gonna believe it is if you check for yourself. Anyway, that's where we last saw Trenton."

Bennett's smirk remained constant while he listened to the accomplice of his main target. "You really must've been in a rush to leave him behind. As you said, double-cross Trenton Loar, you're not gonna like what happens. So, what had you in so much of a hurry that you would put yourself in such a predicament?"

Matt looked at the other mercs, two of whom were eager to inflict torture on the Wynns.

He grumbled, knowing how his answer would be received.

"We have been chased through the forest by Bigfoot."

Bennett stared, completely motionless.

Then, all at once, he and his people started cackling.

"Didn't expect that!" one of them said.

"Should've brought some jerky," another called out.

"Not too late," Bennett replied. "There's a store in town with a big beef jerky sign on the front. We'll have to check it out. But first…" He nodded at the female merc. "Go ahead, Jackson. Let's show Mr. Bing how much we appreciate his sense of humor."

She lowered her rifle, passing it over Bradford's face, neck, chest, stomach, abdomen. Eventually, she got to his knee. There, the rifle muzzle stopped.

He gulped, anticipating a pain he could never have imagined in a million years.

"Howdy!"

"AGH!"

Everyone pivoted, aiming their weapons east, where Trenton Loar himself materialized out of the forest. He snatched up one of the mercenaries by surprise, holding a pistol to his temple while resting the M16 on his shoulder, pointing it at Bennett.

He tipped his head forward to look at his hostage. "Hey there, Gates. How've you been?"

"Good," the merc said through clenched teeth.

"Yeah, you're hating yourself now. I've warned you in the past about maintaining constant awareness."

"Yep."

Trenton looked at the rest of the team.

"Jackson, how's it goin? Donner. Cuomo. Wally." His eyes finished their sweep by locking on to the team leader. "Bennett. Been a while."

"Sure has," his opponent replied. "I see you've been busy."

"I don't like being set up for a hit," Trenton replied. "I figure you of all people can appreciate that."

"I do," Bennett said. "But I've been assigned the task of bringing you down. I'm paid when I see the job through. I figure even you can appreciate *that*."

"That I do," Trenton said. "Doesn't mean I'm gonna take it lying down." He looked at the briefcase on the road. "By the way, holy goddamn! I've gotta hand it to you—and I know it was *your* work. You're always crafting up shit that's outside the box… That diamond tracker. You almost got me with that thing."

Bennett gave a genuine smile. Even at gunpoint, these guys seemed to appreciate each other's talents.

"I'm glad you're impressed."

"Yeah, I even looked through them myself," Trenton continued. "Didn't even pick up on it. I wouldn't have, if you guys weren't flying so damn low. Aside from medevac and police choppers, nobody out this way would fly at such low altitude… unless they were looking for a spot to land. And there's very few reasons why someone would want to land out here."

"Eh!" Bennett kicked a stone, feigning disappointment. "Nobody's perfect, I guess. Though I'm curious: how'd you identify the tracker itself?"

"We were at this big science building—that place Matt was just telling you about. I took a little stroll through one of the labs and checked some of the diamonds with one of their microscopes. Like I said: I'm impressed."

"Wait a minute," Heather said. "You gave the case back to Matt. Then disappeared. You used us for bait?"

"Sorry," Trenton said blankly. "Had to think fast. You know, with all the fun taking place back there."

"Oh, right," Bennett laughed. "Bigfoot. You really are having a bad day, aren't you?"

"I've had better." Trenton took his pistol from Gates' head to pop some sort of treat in his mouth.

"This standoff can't last forever, Trenton," Bennett said. He put his gun to Matt's head. "I might be reaching here, but I've got a job to finish. So, you've got three seconds to surrender, and if you don't we'll kill all three of your pals. You probably won't care, but it's worth a try. I'd rather you don't put a bullet through Gates' head, but you're not getting out of here alive. Shoot him, you have nobody to hide behind. Frankly, I'm shocked you didn't just plant the diamond tracker on Matt and make off with the real ones."

"Thought crossed my mind," Trenton said.

A moment of silence passed, during which Trenton turned his head, listening to something in the woods.

To everyone's surprise, he dropped the M16.

Bennett responded with, "Interesting. What's the catch?"

"No catch," Trenton said, keeping his pistol to Gates' head. "Let them step away, and I'll give myself up."

Some of the mercs sported smiles.

"You have a conscience?" Bennett said. "When did this start?"

"I've killed many people in my day," Trenton said. "So many, I've grown used to it. That said, I've never screwed anyone over to save my own skin. Let them go."

Bennett, interested in this turn of events, nodded at his people. "Go ahead. Let them go."

"Him too?" Jackson asked, looking at Matt.

"Him too," Bennett said.

The three hostages stepped away, keeping their backs to the vehicle.

Trenton moved forward, keeping his hold on Gates. Satisfied with the others being out of the line of fire, he pushed Gates forward. The merc spun around, eager to be the first one to blow holes in their target.

Trenton pointed his pistol skyward and slowly dug into his pocket. "Just some professional courtesy before you do what you have to do…" Bennett waited to give the order, watching Trenton's hand. An open Hershey bar came out of the pocket.

"Got a sweet tooth?" Bennett asked.

Trenton smiled. "The lab back there has a hell of an infirmary. They treat their employees well, especially when it comes to desserts. The place is loaded with all sorts of goodies. Chocolate bars, Reese's cups, M&Ms, Snickers. Gotta be careful though. We're in the woods. The scent of this stuff is like a magnet for bears…"

A series of heavy sounds shook the forest behind him.

Stomp! Stomp! Stomp!

"… or Bigfoot."

A huge impact toppled a tree behind him, making way for the fourteen-foot-tall beast.

Bennett and his team came alive with fright.

"Holy shit!" Bennett pointed his gun. "Weapons free!"

Trenton ran to the side, allowing Bigfoot to do his dirty work for him.

Several rifle rounds tore into the creature. Roaring in pain, Bigfoot charged the team of gunmen.

Gates was immediately snatched off the ground. Those jaws opened wide and closed over his head, biting it clean off and spitting it at the others.

The psychological warfare of seeing their teammate's bloody head rolling like a bowling ball had the intended effect. Their eyes went to the ground, their aim wavering.

Bigfoot came at them, swiping its right arm.

Jackson was the next to be decapitated, her head flying far into the woods. Her body shook, the finger squeezing the rifle's trigger. Understanding the deadly effects of that weapon, Bigfoot quickly grabbed her shoulders and whipped her in the opposite direction.

Wally yelled out, his chest opening up. The bullets from her gun exited out his back, one of them catching Donner in the shoulder. He fell to the pavement, scrambling to get away from the approaching brute.

He repositioned his own weapon and fired off a few rounds. Bigfoot lurched, its own blood spilling from its chest.

All the more pissed, it grabbed the gun and pulled it from the human's grip. Holding it like an icepick, Bigfoot drove it downward, putting its muzzle through Donner's eye socket.

More shots rang out, resulting in blood splattering from between the monster's shoulders.

The beast lurched in pain, then turned around, making eye contact with Bennett.

He aimed high, steadied his hands, and fired another shot.

Bigfoot's head snapped back. A trickle of blood ran down its face. It put its finger to the hole, dislodging the piece of lead lodged against its thick skull.

Bennett's breathing intensified, the futility of his situation growing more apparent.

"Fuck…"

The beast moved in a straight line, smacked the gun from his hand, then lifted him high over its head.

The hardened killer kicked his feet like a child, yelling in pain while Bigfoot slowly bent him backward.

SNAP!

His back went. After that, the monster's hands pulled in opposite directions, separating Bennett's waist and pelvis from the rest of him.

Trenton made his way over to the rest of his group. "You guys alright?"

"Yeah," Bradford said, astonished. "What'd you do?"

"I told the truth." Trenton offered a piece of his Hershey bar. "Having this stuff in the woods is a bad idea. Leaving a trail of it while you plan on foiling your enemy's ambush, totally a bad idea." He tossed the wrapper aside and checked the magazine in his pistol. "Sorry I had to resort to devious means."

"You could've left the tracker back there," Heather said. "Thrown them off."

"I could've. Except that would rely on the hopes they would not track the only vehicle leaving that area, which also only happened to be going at two miles an hour."

Heather went silent, realizing he had a point.

"Thanks for all that exposition," Matt said. "But in case you didn't notice, we're next on the menu!"

Up the road, the beast turned around. It exhaled, bleeding from its face and chest where it had taken numerous bullets.

Unwilling to stop its reign of terror, it began moving down the road, fists clenched.

Trenton rolled into a seated position, placing his magazine into the handle of his gun. "I should also inform you I was aware they'd want to confirm I was dead, and they would want to know what kind of collateral damage there would be. By that, I mean

I knew they wouldn't shoot to kill right away. Not without having a visual on me. And they wouldn't risk exploding the tank, because identifying the bodies would be too much of a pain." He extended his gun. "Which is good, because I needed that tank to wrap things up."

Bigfoot started passing the vehicle, its bloody arm grazing the steel container.

BANG! BANG! BANG!

Every round in the magazine struck the container, exposing the fuel to the air, the sparks igniting it.

A fireball of epic proportions rose from the truck.

All four spectators fell backward, a wave of hot air passing over them. Like rolling thunder, the soundwaves traveled far and wide, the smoke rising into the blue sky.

Bradford sat up.

The flames had spread across the road, consuming the bodies, popping off their ammunition.

Nowhere in those ruins was the beast to be seen.

"Where is it?" Heather said.

"Couldn't tell ya," Bradford said. "The flames are pretty big. Must be in there somewhere. Or maybe blown to bits. Did you see it, Trenton?"

The assassin groaned, his bell rung by the huge explosion. "After the flash, all I saw was the sky and my own big feet." He watched the raging fire. "Can't imagine that sucker shrugging that off, though."

"I don't see a body," Heather said. "I can see the guys who were after you. But I don't see the monster."

Bradford took notice of some small flames far into the woods heading southeast.

"Wait… you think he could've survived?"

"If so, he's not coming back," Trenton said. "That Bigfoot's a tough bastard, but nobody's immune to fire."

"Or the brute force of a propane truck explosion," Heather added.

"Suits me," Matt grumbled. He sat himself up, watching the aftermath of the explosion. Somewhere in that lake of fire was the briefcase. "So much for getting away rich."

Trenton started to chuckle.

"Oh, you think that's funny?" Matt said. "Sixty million dollars, down the tube. I mean, technically the diamonds can't be destroyed in the fire. But that case will be welded shut. Getting them out will take a drill designed for burrowing into…"

A plastic bag fell from Trenton's hand onto his lap. Matt looked down, slowly realizing what was in front of his eyes.

"Wait… oh! You shithead! You did take them out while you were in the lab!"

"Just as a precaution," Trenton said with a laugh.

Matt held the diamonds up to his eyes, then started laughing. "So, you're still good with the plan?"

Trenton nodded. "I know you've been wanting to get out of the business and start a new life. I'm not a good guy, and there's no escaping that. Maybe I don't deserve to get away with everything I've done. But you're redeemable. You've got your whole life ahead of you. Do something good with it."

It wasn't something he expected to hear from a hitman of all people, but Matt appreciated those words all the same.

The two criminals stood up and looked to their new friends.

"Bradford, Heather…" Matt said.

"Good to meet ya," Trenton said. "Stay here. Someone'll be flying by to investigate this fire."

Bradford gave them a farewell wave. "Good luck."

"And try not to encounter any more forest monsters," Heather added.

Smiling in response to that, the two men disappeared into the woods in pursuit of a new future. It would be a long and hard journey, especially on foot, but something in Bradford's gut told him they would make it.

Heather took his hand. "After we finish explaining this whole thing to the police, would you like to go on a new trip?"

Bradford squeezed her hand. "Preferably somewhere indoors."

Beaming smiles, they pressed their lips together.

Trenton and Matt may have gotten away filthy rich, but Bradford and Heather Wynn were the ones who felt truly wealthy.

The End

Check out other great

Cryptid Novels!

Hunter Shea

THE DOVER DEMON

The Dover Demon is real...and it has returned. In 1977, Sam Brogna and his friends came upon a terrifying, alien creature on a deserted country road. What they witnessed was so bizarre, so chilling, they swore their silence. But their lives were changed forever. Decades later, the town of Dover has been hit by a massive blizzard. Sam's son, Nicky, is drawn to search for the infamous cryptid, only to disappear into the bowels of a secret underground lair. The Dover Demon is far deadlier than anyone could have believed. And there are many of them. Can Sam and his reunited friends rescue Nicky and battle a race of creatures so powerful, so sinister, that history itself has been shaped by their secretive presence? "THE DOVER DEMON is Shea's most delightful and insidiously terrifying monster yet." – Shotgun Logic Reviews "An excellent horror novel and a strong standout in the UFO and cryptid subgenres." –Hellnotes "Non-stop action awaits those brave enough to dive into the small town of Dover, and if you're lucky, you won't see the Demon himself!" – The Scary Reviews PRAISE FOR SWAMP MONSTER MASSACRE "B-horror movie fans rejoice, Hunter Shea is here to bring you the ultimate tale of terror!" – Horror Novel Reviews "A nonstop thrill ride! I couldn't put this book down." – Cedar Hollow Horror Reviews

Armand Rosamilia

THE BEAST

The end of summer, 1986. With only a few days left until the new school year, twins Jeremy and Jack Schaffer are on very different paths. Jeremy is the geek, playing Dungeons & Dragons with friends Kathleen and Randy, while Jack is the jock, getting into trouble with his buddies. And then everything changes when neighbor Mister Higgins is killed by a wild animal in his yard. Was it a bear? There's something big lurking in the woods behind their New Jersey home.Will the police be able to solve the murder before more Middletown residents are ripped apart?

Check out other great

Cryptid Novels!

Edward J. McFadden III

THE CRYPTID CLUB

When cryptozoologist Ash Cohn receives a gold embossed printed invitation inviting him to join The Cryptid Club, he sees the resolution to all his problems.Famous cryptid scientist and biologist, Lester Treemont, one of the world's richest men, and the leader of the Cryptid Club, is dying. What he offers via his invitation is a chance to succeed him. To take over his wealth, laboratory, and discoveries. All Ash has to do is beat eight others like him in a series of tests both mental and physical involving Treemont's collection of cryptids. Seems simple enough, and Ash has nothing to lose.Nine strangers from across the globe, all with reasons for wanting to win. When they start dying one by one, the competition shifts to one of survival. Who among them will rise to the top and reign over The Cryptid Club?

William Meikle

INFESTATION

It was supposed to be a simple mission. A suspected Russian spy boat is in trouble in Canadian waters. Investigate and report are the orders. But when Captain John Banks and his squad arrive, it is to find an empty vessel, and a scene of bloody mayhem. Soon they are in a fight for their lives, for there are things In the icy seas off Baffin Island, scuttling, hungry things with a taste for human flesh. They are swarming. And they are growing. "Scotland's best Horror writer" - Ginger Nuts of Horror "The premier storyteller of our time." - Famous Monsters of Filmland